A bright energy infused her veins. For the first time in her life, there was someone who understood her, who encouraged her. On an impulse, she threw herself at him. Arms wrapped around his neck, she pressed a hard kiss to his cheek. It lasted only a few seconds, half a minute at the most.

And yet, she couldn't forget the steely cage of his arms around her waist.

Pulling away, she refused to look at him.

In her wardrobe, she pulled out a knee-length, sleeveless cream silk dress, one of the classiest creations she'd ever seen.

The dress slithered over her skin with a soft whisper. But she couldn't get the back zipper all the way.

Face frozen into an unaffected smile, she walked back out and presented her back to him. "Zip me up."

An aeon seemed to pass before he tugged the zipper up, and another eternity when the pads of his fingers lingered on the nape of her neck.

"Do I look good enough to be Mrs. Vittori now?"

Conveniently Wed!

Conveniently wedded, passionately bedded!

Whether there's a debt to be paid, a will to be obeyed or a business to be saved...she's got no choice but to say, "I do!"

But these billionaire bridegrooms have got another think coming if they imagine marriage will be that easy...

Soon their convenient brides become the objects of inconvenient desire!

Find out what happens after the vows in:

Look out for more Conveniently Wed! stories coming soon!

Tara Pammi

—

SICILIAN'S BRIDE FOR A PRICE

Recycling programs
for this product may
not exist in your area.

ISBN-13: 978-1-335-41984-2

Sicilian's Bride for a Price

First North American publication 2018

Copyright © 2018 by Tara Pammi

Printed in U.S.A.

Tara Pammi can't remember a moment when she wasn't lost in a book—especially a romance, which was much more exciting than a mathematics textbook at school. Years later, Tara's wild imagination and love for the written word revealed what she really wanted to do. Now she pairs alpha males who think they know everything with strong women who knock that theory and them off their feet!

Books by Tara Pammi

Harlequin Presents

The Sheikh's Pregnant Prisoner

Conveniently Wed!

Bought with the Italian's Ring
Blackmailed by the Greek's Vows

The Drakon Royals

Crowned for the Drakon Legacy
The Drakon Baby Bargain
His Drakon Runaway Bride

Brides for Billionaires

Married for the Sheikh's Duty

The Legendary Conti Brothers

The Surprise Conti Child
The Unwanted Conti Bride

Greek Tycoons Tamed

Claimed for His Duty
Bought for Her Innocence

Visit the Author Profile page
at Harlequin.com for more titles.

For my very own hero, my husband, Raghu.
Twenty is nothing—I could write a hundred heroes
inspired by you.

CHAPTER ONE

DANTE VITTORI STARED at the legal document that had been delivered an hour ago. The floor-to-ceiling glass windows that made up three whole sides of his office on the forty-sixth floor of Matta Towers in Central London cast the luxurious space in an orange glow, thanks to the setting sun behind him.

Vikram Matta—his mentor Neel Matta's son and Dante's best friend—was now legally dead.

He felt a twinge in his chest for exactly one minute.

He'd learned that grief, like regret, was a useless emotion. He'd learned this at the age of thirteen when his father had killed himself instead of facing lifelong incarceration for his Ponzi scheme that had fleeced hundreds of people. He'd learned this when his mother had simply changed her name back to her Sicilian father's and married a man he approved of within a year of his father's death.

Giving in to his emotions would have crushed Dante back then. Vikram was gone; he'd made his peace with it a long time ago.

Quickly, he rifled through the documents, to ensure he hadn't missed anything.

He was almost to the last couple of pages when he stilled.

Voting Shares of the Deceased

The hairs at the back of his neck prickled. His mind instantly rewound back to the conversation he and Vikram had had with Neel when Neel had found he hadn't much time to live.

Neel Matta had started Matta Steel, a small steel manufacturing business, almost forty years ago, but it was Dante who had grown it into the billion-dollar conglomerate it was now. Against his own brother, Nitin's wishes, for the first time in the history of the company, Neel had granted his own voting shares to Dante, an outsider.

He had made Dante a part of his family. And now Matta Steel was the blood in his veins, his mistress, his everything.

Instead of wasting time grieving after Neel's death and Vikram's horrific plane crash, Dante had taken the company from strength to strength, cementing his position as the CEO.

But with Vikram's voting shares being up for grabs now...

His secretary, Izzy, came into the office without knocking. Being another alum of Neel Matta's generosity, Izzy took for granted a certain personal privilege with Dante that he didn't allow anyone else. Neither did he doubt that she'd interrupted him for a good reason.

The redhead's gaze flew to the papers in front of him, clear distress in those green eyes for a moment. But when she met his gaze, she was the consummate professional.

Of course Vikram's death had touched her too, but like him, Izzy was nothing if not practical.

Pushing his chair back, he laced his fingers at the back of his neck and said, "Spill it."

"I heard from Nitin's secretary, Norma, that he's thinking of calling an emergency board meeting with special counsel present."

Neel's brother was so predictable in his greed and deception. "I was expecting that."

"I wasn't sure if you had realized it has to do with Vicky's voting shares being up for grabs now."

"I did." Izzy was both competent and brilliant. And utterly loyal to him. The one quality he knew he couldn't buy even with his billions. "Tell me your thoughts."

She took a seat and opened her notebook. "I pressed a little on Norma and learned that he means to go over the bylaws in front of the board and direct the conclusion that Vikram's shares—" an infinitesimal catch in her throat again "—should go to him, since the bylaws state that the voting shares are to be kept in the family."

"Except when Neel modified them to grant me his shares." They had been a gift when Dante had made a big business win. Neel had been paving his way into retirement, wanting to slow down and let Dante take over. Instead his heart disease had killed him in a matter of months.

"He means to censure that as an aberration on Neel's part due to his ailing health."

Dante smiled. "It's an allegation he's continued to make for nigh on ten years now, even though I have held the controlling stake in the company."

"Also, he's conveniently forgotten Ali."

For the first time in years, Dante found his thoughts in sudden disarray.

His mentor's rebel daughter had always been the one thorn in his rise to success. The one piece of trouble in Neel's life that Dante hadn't solved for the man he'd worshipped. The one element he'd never quite figured out properly.

"No, he hasn't." Alisha's scorn for her father's company wasn't a secret.

He stood up from his seat. London's night was glittering into life all around them. "Nitin's counting on Ali simply refusing to have anything to do with the company, as always. Which means he can inherit all of Vikram's shares."

"Can't you contest that?"

"I can, but if he gets the board on his side and they rule that the shares go to him, there's not a lot I can do. He'd own the majority. Unless I got…" He trailed off, an idea occurring to him. "Nitin needs to be taught the lesson that I own Matta Steel. Irrevocably."

"I'm assuming you've already come up with a plan for that."

He had. A brilliant one. He hadn't put his heart and

blood and soul into Matta Steel just so he'd have to defend it every other year.

Again, that twinge of doubt pulled at his chest. He flicked it away. There was no room for emotions in his decision. The only thing he would never violate was Neel's trust in him—and that meant keeping control of Matta Steel.

Alisha had never wanted to be a part of her papa's legacy. She had turned her back on everything to do with the company and Neel and even Vikram when he'd been alive.

She'd had nothing but resentment for Dante for as long as he could remember. And he would feel no compunction in taking the things he wanted—the things that she scorned anyway—off her hands, forever.

All he needed was leverage.

Everyone had a price and he just needed to find Ali's. "Find out where she's holed up now. She could be anywhere."

Izzy jerked her head up, shock dancing in her green eyes. "Ali?"

There was reluctance, maybe even unwillingness in her stare.

"Yes. Find Alisha," he said, simply dismissing the unasked question in Izzy's eyes. He pulled his jacket on and checked his phone. No reason for him to miss out on his date with the latest Broadway actress touring London.

He reached the door and then turned. "Oh, also, call that PI for me, won't you? I want to have a little chat with him."

"Which one?"

"The one I have on my payroll to keep track of Alisha's movements."

"But you never look at his reports." Izzy's accusation was clear. He'd never given a damn about Alisha except to have someone keep an eye on her, for the purpose of extricating her if she got herself into trouble.

For Neel's sake.

"I didn't need to, until now. She's been safe, mostly, *si*?" It was a miracle in itself, since she traveled through all the hellholes of the world in the name of her little hobby. Izzy didn't need to know he read every single one of those reports. On any given day, he knew how and where Alisha was. "Now, however, I need a little bit more info on her."

"Dante—"

"None of your business, Isabel." He cut her off smoothly and closed the door behind him.

Izzy had been the one constant person in his life for so long, from the moment he had come to live with Neel all those years ago, yes. But it didn't mean he invited her into his private thoughts or that he considered her a personal friend.

Dante Vittori didn't do relationships, of any kind.

"There's someone here to see you, Ali."

Alisha Matta looked up from her crouch on the floor of the Grand Empire Palace restaurant. Her shoulders were tight from supporting the weight of the camera and her thighs burned at her continued position. Ignoring her friend Mak's voice, she kept clicking.

She'd been waiting all morning in the small kitchen of the crowded restaurant, waiting for Kiki to come home.

The pop of the flash of her Nikon sang through her nerves, the few moments of clarity and purpose making the wait of the last three months utterly worth it. "To your right, look into the camera. No, jut your left hip out, you're gorgeous, Kiki," she continued the words of encouragement. She'd managed to learn a little Thai in the last year but her stuttering accent had only made Kiki laugh.

The neon lights and the cheap pink linoleum floors became the perfect background as Kiki shed her jeans and shirt in a move that was both efficient and sensual as hell. Her lithe dancer's body sang for the camera.

But even the perfection of the shot couldn't stop the distraction of Mak hovering.

"If it's John, tell him we're done," she whispered.

"It's an Italian gentleman. In a three-piece Tom Ford suit that I'm pretty sure is custom designed and black handmade Italian loafers. Gucci, I think."

Ali fell back onto her haunches with a soft thud, hanging on to her expensive camera for dear life. Mak was crazy about designer duds. There was only one Italian gentleman she knew. Except, if it was who she thought it was, he shouldn't be called a gentleman. More a ruthless soul in the garb of one.

"Said his name was..."

Ali's heart thudded in tune with the loud blare of the boom box. "What, Mak?"

Mak scrunched his brow. "You know, the guy who wrote about all those circles of hell, that one."

"Dante," Ali whispered the word softly. How appropriate that Mak would mention Dante and hell in the same sentence.

Because that was what her papa's protégé represented to her.

The very devil from hell.

Princesses in glass castles shouldn't throw stones, bella.

Okay, yes, devil was a bit overboard because he hadn't actually ever harmed Ali, but still, Ali hated him.

So what was the devil, whose usual playground was the London social circuit, doing on the other side of the world in Bangkok?

The last time they had laid eyes on each other had been when she'd learned of Vikram's plane crash. She closed her eyes, fighting the memory of the disastrous night, but it came anyway.

She'd been so full of rage, so vulnerable and so vicious toward Dante. For no reason except that he was alive while her brother was gone. Gone before she could reconnect with him.

"He doesn't look like he's happy to be kept waiting," Mak interrupted her trip down a nightmarish memory lane.

Ali pulled herself up.

No, super busy billionaire Dante Vittori wouldn't like waiting in the ramshackle hotel. How impatient he must be to get back to his empire. To his billions.

How dare Ali keep him waiting while each minute

of his time could mean another deal he could broker, another billion he could add to his pile, another company he... She smiled wide.

She'd make him wait.

Because Dante being here meant only one thing: he needed something from her.

And she would jump through those nine circles of hell before she did anything that made his life easier. Or calmer. Or richer.

Slowly, with shaking fingers, she packed up her camera. She pulled the strap of the bag over her shoulder, picked up her other paraphernalia, kissed Kiki's cheek and pushed the back door open.

The late September evening was balmy, noisy and full of delicious smells emanating from all the restaurants that lined up the street.

Her stomach growled. She promised herself some authentic pad thai and a cold can of Coke as soon as she got to her flat. Thwarting Dante and a well-earned dinner suddenly seemed like a highly pleasurable way to spend her day.

Just as she took another step into the busy street, a black chauffeur-driven Mercedes pulled up, blocking her. Ali blinked at her reflection in the polished glass of the window when the door opened. Out stepped Dante.

In his crisp white shirt, which did wonders for his olive complexion, and tailored black pants, he looked like he'd stepped out of a *GQ* magazine cover and casually strolled into the colorful street.

His Patek Philippe watch—a gift from her father

when he'd welcomed Dante onto the board of Matta
Steel, yet one more thing Papa had given Dante and
not her—gleamed on his wrist as he stood leaning
carelessly against the door, a silky smile curving that
sculpted mouth. "Running away again, Alisha?"

He was the only one who insisted on calling her
Alisha. Somehow he managed to fill it with reprimand
and contempt.

All thoughts of pad thai were replaced with the cold
burn of resentment as that penetrating gaze took in her
white spaghetti strap top and forest green shorts and
traveled from her feet in flip-flops to her hair bunched
into a messy bun on top of her head. It was dismissive
and yet so thorough that her skin prickled.

Chin tilted, Ali stared right back. She coated it in
defiance but after so long, she was greedy for the sight
of him. Shouts from street vendors and the evening
bustle faded out.

A careless heat filled her veins as she noted the aris-
tocratic nose—broken in his adolescence and fixed—
the dark, stubble-coated line of his jaw and deep-set
eyes that always mocked her, the broad reach of his
shoulders, the careless arrogance that filled every pore.
He exuded that kind of masculine confidence that announced him as the top of the food chain both in the
boardroom and out of it.

And his mouth… The upper lip was thin and carved
and the lower was fuller and lush, the only hint of soft-
ness in that face and body. It was a soft whisper about
the sensuality he buried under that ruthlessness.

Her heart was now thundering in her chest, not unlike Mak's boom box. Heat flushed her from within. She jerked her gaze to meet his, saw the slight flare of his nostrils.

Christ, what was she doing? What was she imagining?

Ali moved her tongue around in her dry mouth, and somehow managed to say, "I have nothing to say and I want nothing to do with you."

To do with you...

The words mocked her, mocked the adolescent infatuation she'd nursed for him that she now hated, morphing into something much worse. Everything she despised about him also attracted her to him. If that weren't a red flag...

He halted her dignified exit with his fingers on her wrist, the calloused pads of his fingers playing on her oversensitized skin.

She jerked her arm out of his grip like a scalded cat. His mouth tightened, but whatever emotion she had incited disappeared behind his controlled mask. "I have a proposal that I'm sure you would like to hear."

God, how she wanted to do or say something that made that mask shatter completely. How she wished she could be the one who brought the arrogant man to his knees. Her sudden bloodthirstiness shocked even her.

She'd always liked coloring outside the lines, yes, but not to the point of self-destruction. And that was what Dante made her do. Always.

At some point, hating him had become more important than trying to build a bridge to her father, than reconnecting with Vikram.

No more.

No playing to his point by doing something he would hate; no trying to stir up that smooth facade and burn her bridges.

You're a necessary nuisance, Alisha. I put up with your mind games for his sake. Only for his.

A calm filled her at her resolution. "What do you want from me?"

A brow rose in the too angular face. There was that tightness to his mouth again. In a parallel universe, Ali would have concluded that that assumption pricked him. In this one where she knew Dante Vittori had no emotions, she didn't.

"Why are you so sure that I want something from you?"

"You're thousands of miles away from your empire. From everything I know, there's no steel plant in this area, nor a lot of demand for it. Unless you're scouting the area to build a new plant with cheap labor, then you're not to check up on me."

"I've always known where you are, Alisha."

She swallowed.

"However much you like to pretend that there are no ties between us, however far you run in pursuit of your little hobby, you are, at the end of the day, his daughter."

His statement put paid to any emotional extrapolation she was still stupid enough to make from his previous one. As if he worried she might read too much—or anything at all—into him keeping tabs on her.

He had always been loyal to her father; would always be loyal to him. Keeping track of her fell somewhere under that umbrella. Nothing at all to do with the woman she was.

Nothing.

"I'm not interested in trading insults with you," she said, unable to stop her voice from cracking. "I'm not... I'm not that impulsive, destructive Ali anymore."

"That would be a nice change of pace for us, *si*? So we'll have dinner and not trade insults tonight."

"I said no insults. That doesn't mean I want to be anywhere near you for more than five minutes." It was her own confused emotions and this...blasted attraction that made her want to avoid him even now.

"Ah..." With a graceful flick of his wrist, he made a big show of checking his watch. "That lasted about thirty seconds." His gaze caught hers. "I'm not and have never been your enemy, Alisha."

And just like that, her attraction to him became a near tangible thing in the air. Her hating him became the only weapon in her armor. "Eating out is a pleasure for me and somehow I don't see that being the primary emotion if we're forced together for too long."

A calculating glint appeared in his eyes. "There's something you want in my grasp. When will you learn to act guided by your goals and not by your emotions?"

She could feel herself shaking. "Not everyone is an ambitious, heartless bastard like you are." There went her resolution to be polite. "Just tell me what your proposal is. Now."

"It has to do with your mother's charity. That's all you'll get now. My chauffeur will pick you up at six for dinner. And, Alisha, dress appropriately. We won't be eating hunched over some street vendor's stall in the market. Neither will I appreciate the half-naked, wrapped-around-a-has-been-rock-star look you sported the last time around for my benefit."

How she wished she could say it hadn't been for his benefit, but they both knew it had been. Her eighteenth and his twenty-eighth birthday party would be etched on her memory forever.

"Arrogant, ruthless, manipulative, controlling, yes, but I never thought you were a snob," she threw back at him.

"Because I want to have a civilized dinner at a place where you won't throw things at me?"

Another bad night. Another bad memory.

No, it was time to rewrite how Dante saw her. Time to stop expecting things from him from some unwritten script in her own head. "One dinner. No more."

She'd almost walked away.

"Why does it bother you so much to be around me?"

Her face burned and it had nothing to do with the last of the day's heat. "It doesn't."

"*No?* Isn't that why you avoid your family home, why you never come to London? You avoid your extended family, your old friends, you move from place to place like a nomad."

You took everything that should have been mine, she wanted to say, like she'd done once. But it wouldn't be the truth.

Dante hadn't taken anything her father hadn't been more than happy and willing to give him. Dante hadn't shattered her family. Her father had.

But when it came to him...she was still that morass of anger and attraction and something more that she was terrified to discover. "That mansion, even London, they haven't been home to me in a long time."

That silky, slick smile tugged up the corners of his mouth again. "It's a relief to know then that your life's not revolved around avoiding me then, *si*. See you tonight, Alisha."

He was gone before she could blink, before she could counter the arrogant assumption. As she went home, Ali couldn't shake off the sense of dread that settled in her gut.

She and Dante couldn't stand each other. So why the hell was he insisting on an intimate dinner? And how would she get through it without compromising her dignity?

CHAPTER TWO

OF COURSE THE infuriating man couldn't simply text her the name of the hotel when he'd ordered her to dress appropriately, Ali thought, as the black Mercedes weaved through the heavy traffic, leaving the bustle of the city behind.

But having known Dante since the age of twelve, Ali had made a guess.

Dante was a man who expected, no, *demanded* the best of everything in life. He had a reputation for being a perfectionist with his employees but then no one complained because he rewarded hard work and ambition. God, she'd really gone looking for reasons to hate him back then.

The luxury Mercedes pulled smoothly into the courtyard of the latest on-trend, five-star resort that had been renovated last year to look like it could proudly belong in any posh European city, with the boat-filled canals of the Chao Phraya river offering a lovely view. The seafood at the restaurant was to die for, Mak had informed her, and he'd heard it from one of his many connections in high places.

Okay, so the worst thing that could come of this meeting was that she could walk away having had a delicious dinner at a lovely restaurant. And to prove to Dante that she could fake class and poise with the best of them.

She smoothed her hand over her stomach as she stepped out of the car and was pleased with the light pink sheath dress that she'd chosen to calm the butterflies. In the guise of studying the hotel's striking exterior, she took a moment to study herself in the reflection of the glass facade.

Her long hair, freshly washed and blow-dried to within an inch of its life, fell to her waist like a dark silky curtain, her only jewelry a thin gold chain with a tiny diamond disappearing into the low V-neck of her dress. The linen dress was a cheap knockoff of a designer brand she couldn't afford on her erratic income. But she looked like a million bucks, the fabric clinging to every dip and rise of her toned body as if it were custom designed for her.

The light pink was set off perfectly against her dusky skin and she'd let Kiki do her makeup—smoky eyes, gold bronzer and pale pink lip gloss. Tonight, she would be the sophisticated, poised Ali her mother had raised her to be, even if it killed her.

Another glance at the financial papers of her mother's charity hadn't changed reality. Other than a huge influx of cash, there was nothing anyone could do to save it. So, if Dante had something that could help, Ali would listen. She would treat this as a meeting with a professional.

Her beige pumps click-clacked on the gleaming

cream marble floor as she walked up to the entrance
to the restaurant. Soft yellow light fell from contem-
porary chrome fixtures. Beige walls and cream leather
chairs gave the restaurant an utterly decadent, romantic atmosphere. Her belly swooped as Ali caught sight
of Dante's bent head, the thick jet-black hair glittering
in the lights.

Gripping her clutch tighter, Ali looked around. Every
other table was empty. She checked her knockoff watch
and saw it was only seven in the evening, nowhere near
closing time.

The setting was far too intimate, far too private. Just
far too much a scene plucked right out of her adolescent
fantasies. But before she could turn tail and run out of
the restaurant, that jet-black gaze caught her.

The mockery in those eyes made Ali straighten her
shoulders and put one foot in front of the other.

He stood up when she reached their booth—a cocoon of privacy in an already silent restaurant. He'd ex-
changed the white shirt for a slate-gray one that made
his eyes pop. With his jaw freshly shaved, thick dark
hair slicked back half-wet, he was so…no, handsome
was a lukewarm word for Dante's fierce masculinity.

The scent of his aftershave, with an aqua note to it,
was subtle, but combined with the warmth of his skin, it
sank into Ali's pores. Every cell in her body came alive.

"Where is everybody?"

"Everybody?" he said, standing far too close for her
sanity.

Ali sat down with a plop, hand smoothing over her
stomach. "Yes, people. Other Homo sapiens. Who might

want to partake of the delicious food I've heard they serve here."

There was no mockery now when he looked down at her.

Heat swarming her cheeks, Ali ran her fingers through her hair. "What?"

His gaze swept over her face, her hair, the low V-neckline, but went no farther down. A shiver clamped her spine. "You clean up nice."

"Oh." The one syllable hung in the air, and she looked away, pretending to smooth her dress, putting her clutch down.

He took his sweet time sitting down, not opposite her, but on the side of the table, to her left. Ali shifted her knees away to the far right.

"If you scoot any farther down, you'll fall off the seat. Why are you so jumpy?"

Ali stilled, clasped her restless fingers in her lap. "I'm not."

"*No?* Really?"

His accent got thicker any time he got a little emotional. It was one of the tells Ali had picked up a long time ago. Pulling herself together, she met his gaze. Did he really have no idea what being near him did to her equilibrium? Did he really not feel the charge in the air around them, the pulse of undercurrents in every word, every look…? God, how was it that she was the only one who felt so much?

Not that she wanted Dante to be attracted to her. Her shoulders shook as a shiver of another kind traveled down her spine.

"If you're jumpy around me, it means you've arranged a little something for me. A surprise."

Ah...that was what he attributed it to. She closed her eyes and counted to ten. She couldn't even blame him because back then she'd been a little devil all right.

She'd lit sparklers in his room one Diwali night that had put holes in the new suit her papa had bought him. And that had almost lit the entire house on fire.

She'd taken a hammer to his new cuff links—Vikram's present—and minced them to so much dust.

Oh, and let's not forget the documents for an important merger she'd taken from his room and shredded.

When he'd brought his girlfriend to meet her papa... Ali groaned at the memory. And those weren't the half of all the destructive things she'd done to show how much she hated him.

She cleared her throat. "I told you. I've changed." When he raised a brow, she sighed. "I didn't know where we were dining. How could I arrange anything? I was just surprised to see no other patrons, that's all."

"I had my secretary book the entire restaurant for us." When her mouth fell open, he shrugged. "If you were going to cause a public scene—which given my knowledge of your character seemed like a high probability—I wanted to minimize the public part."

"Fair enough," she replied back with all the sass she could manage. Other people would have been a buffer, other people would have distracted her from this...whatever made her skin prickle with awareness.

Luckily, before her sudden awkwardness could betray her, the maître d' arrived.

"A bottle of your best white wine and the shrimp salad for both of us."

Ali lifted her chin. "I don't want shrimp."

"No?"

His fingers touched her wrist, and again, Ali pulled back as if he were a live current.

His jaw tightened, a flare of heat in his eyes. "Even though it's what this restaurant is famous for and you made that soft moan when your eyes came to that item on the menu?"

Her cheeks aflame, her heart pounding, Ali stared down at the menu. The words blurred, the tension between them winding round and round.

"Madam?" His expression set into a pleasing smile, the maître d' spoke up. "If you don't want the seafood that Mr. Vittori has ordered," he said, "might I suggest something else?"

"No." Ali took a deep breath. It wasn't the poor man's fault that Dante was playing with her. And she had played into his hands like she was still that irrational, impulsive hothead who wanted to hurt him for everything that was wrong in her world. "I'll have the shrimp, thanks."

"Don't," she simply said, once the man left.

Don't manipulate me. Don't rub me the wrong way. Just don't...be in my life.

Dante leaned back, his stare intense. "Don't make it so easy."

Before Ali could launch into another argument, he placed a rectangular velvet case on the table. Ten minutes into the dinner and she felt like she was already emotionally wound up. She fell back against her seat. Of course, he was the master manipulator, playing on weaknesses, while he had remained untouchable.

"What now?"

"Open it."

Just get it over with. Just get it over with. And walk away.

Ali opened the clasp. She caught sight of the tiny, exquisitely cut diamonds set into flowers with such delicate white gold that it always took her breath away, as it glittered under the soft lights. She rubbed the necklace back and forth with the pads of her fingers, compulsively, a balloon of ache in her chest. As if the gentle love of the woman who had worn them might have rubbed off on the stones.

It had taken everything she'd had in her to sell her mother's precious piece.

She pulled the box to her and clasped it so tightly that her knuckles showed white.

First, he had dropped the word about her mother's charity, now the necklace. Dante never did anything without some kind of payoff. He hated her just as much as she did him, and still he had sought her out. The hair on the nape of her neck prickled while her belly went on a swan dive.

"Why do you have this? What do you want, Dante?"

What do you want, Dante?

Dante stared at the tears shimmering in Alisha's large brown eyes, his breath punching into his throat.

It *was* the equivalent of a punch to his gut. He had

borne enough of those in Sicily in his teenage years.
Boys he'd known all his life had turned against Dante
overnight; calling him names, roughing him up.

All thanks to his father's crime.

Those boys' punches had lit a fire in him back then,
fueling his ambition to build a name for himself, sepa-
rate from his father's. They had turned his young heart
into a stone that never felt hurt again.

He had craved a fortune and a name all of his own.
He had decided never to be weak like that again; never
to be at anyone's mercy, least of all be controlled by a
woman's love. And he had turned it into reality.

But the candid emotion in Alisha's face as she
touched her mother's necklace, the havoc it wreaked
on him, was a thousand times worse than any harm that
had been inflicted on his teenage self.

When he'd delved into those reports on Alisha, he'd
been shocked to find that Alisha had visited London
several times over the last five years.

She'd had to go to London to deal with problems
concerning her mother's charity. She had even spear-
headed a charity gala to raise money. He'd been looking for leverage and he had found it.

He wasn't cheating Alisha out of anything she
wanted. He was, in fact, proposing he give her what
she wanted out of it, the one thing she held precious in
return for what he wanted.

No, what threw him into the kind of emotional tur-
moil that he'd always avoided like the plague was that
he was involving *her* in this play.

Alisha, who was a mass of contradictions, who he'd

never quite figured out, who'd been the kind of flighty, selfish, uncaring kind of woman he loathed, was an unknown.

From the moment she'd come to live with her father, Neel, she'd hated Dante with an intensity that he'd first found amusing and then dangerous. Even worse, she'd always incited a reaction in him that no one else provoked.

But all this was before the changes in her the last six years had wrought.

Cristo, the sight of her walking into the back alley a few hours ago—the white spaghetti top plastered to her breasts, her shorts showing off miles and miles of toned legs, the utter sensuality of her movements as she pushed away tendrils of hair falling on her face, the sparkle of the fading sun on her brown skin…

The shock in her face, the greedy, hungry way she'd let those big brown eyes run all over him…even that hadn't made a dent in the need that had pulsed through him.

Dios mio, *this was Neel's daughter.*

She was forbidden to him. And not just because he was determined to take the last bit of her father's legacy from her. But because, with everything he planned to put into motion, Alisha would be the variable. His attraction to her was a weakness he couldn't indulge, much less act on. There were only two positions for women in his life: colleagues like Izzy and a couple of his business associates, women whose judgment he respected, women he genuinely liked; and then there were women he slept with who knew the score, and didn't want more from him.

Alisha didn't fall into either of those camps.

"Dante? What the hell are you doing with my mother's necklace?"

"I bought it back from the guy you sold it to." He made a vague motion to her tears, more shocked than discomfited by them. He'd never seen her as anything but poised to fight her father, him, Vikram, with all guns blazing. Never in this...fragile light. "Looks like I made the right call in thinking you would like it back. Why did you sell it?"

She took another longing look at the box before pushing it back toward him. "For a pair of Jimmy Choos."

"Don't be flippant, Alisha. I never understood why you were always so determined to be your own worst enemy."

"I have no idea what you're talking about. And really, did you invite me to dinner just to point out my flaws?"

He forced himself to pull his gaze from the way she chewed on her lower lip. Suddenly, everything about her—her mind, her body, *Dio*...everything—felt fascinating. Everything was distracting. "I know your mother's charity is failing. Why didn't you come to me for help?"

"Why didn't I come to you for help?" Some of that natural fight in her crawled back into her shoulders. He liked her better like that. He didn't want a vulnerable Alisha on his hands for the next few months. She laughed. White teeth flashed in that gamine face. "Have you met me? And you?"

Despite himself, Dante smiled.

He'd forgotten how witty Alisha could be, how she'd always laughed in any situation, how even with all her tantrums and drama she'd made the house lively when she'd come to live with Neel after her mother's death. Even with grief painting her eyes sad, she'd been so full of life, so full of character, even at the age of twelve.

He'd never gravitated to her, true, but when she'd blossomed into a teenager, it had seemed as if her hatred for him had grown too. The more he had tried to fix things between her and her father, the more she had resented him.

Her gaze slipped to his mouth for a fraction of a second. Every muscle in him tightened. "I'd starve before I take anything from the company. Or you."

He was far too familiar with that spiel to question it now. "What did you need the money for?"

"If you know I sold it, and to whom, then you know why. Come on, Dante, enough beating around the bush."

The waiter brought their food and she thanked him.

She dug into the food with the same intensity with which she seemed to attack everything in life.

Dante, mostly because of the jet lag, pushed his food around. He watched her as she sipped her wine, her tongue flicking out to lick a drop from her lower lip.

He wanted to lick it with his own.

The thought came out of nowhere, hard and fast.

He pushed a hand through his hair and cursed under his breath.

Maledizione! In all the scenarios he had foreseen for this, he hadn't counted how strikingly gorgeous Alisha had become. Or the intensity of the pull he felt toward her.

Whatever tension had been filling up the air, it now filled his veins. And he realized it was because she wasn't focused on him anymore.

Not so with him. Not even the constant reminder, the ironclad self-discipline that made him a revered name in his business circles, the one that told him this was nothing but a quid pro quo, could distract his gaze from the expanse of smooth brown skin her dress exposed. He took the wine flute in his hands, turned it around and around, watching his fingers leaving marks against the condensation.

He wanted to trace his finger against the slope of her shoulders to see if her skin was as silky as it looked. He wanted to touch the pulse at her throat, to sink his fingers into her silky hair and pull her to him, hold her against his body as he plundered her mouth…

She put her fork and spoon down, and took another sip of her wine. Then she leaned back all the way into her seat, her head thrown back over the top. The deep breath she took sent her chest rising and falling.

Basta! He needed to direct this conversation back to his plan.

"Tell me what you've been up to in the last few years." The words slipped out of his mouth. She looked just as shocked as he felt. "You know, other than living like a hobo and moving around every few months."

She shrugged, and the simple gold chain she wore glimmered against her throat, the pendant dangling between her breasts playing peekaboo with him. "You don't have to pretend an interest, Dante. Not now."

"You're his daughter. I've always been interested in what you do with your life. Until I realized my interest only spurred you toward destruction."

"Water under the bridge." She put her napkin on the table, her expression cycling from wariness to fake cheer. "Thank you for the dinner. That was a treat, even with your company. And on second thought, thanks for buying my mother's necklace back." She took the velvet box from him and put it underneath her clutch on the table. Waggling her brows, she leveled a saccharine smile at him. "You must know me well to give me a present I would so appreciate."

Being on the receiving end of that smile was just so… jarring. "You mean to sell it again, don't you?"

"Yep."

"That will only take care of the payroll for another month. I've seen the financials, Alisha. The charity will be bankrupt in a month."

Her mouth tightened. "I'll find a way. I always do."

"Or you could just ask me for help."

"I told you, I don't want your money. Or the company's or Papa's. I need to do this on my own."

"Does the charity home really mean that much to you?"

"It does. It's where Mama grew up. I spent so much

time there with her. Some of the happiest moments of my childhood were there."

"If you really want to save the home, put aside your irrational resentment of me and I will funnel some much needed money into it."

"And what do I have to do in return?"

"Marry me."

CHAPTER THREE

MARRY ME...

Marry Dante...

Ali's mind went into a loop over that one phrase, like one of those gramophone records her mama had had.

Marry Dante, marry Dante...

Dante, who thought she was selfish and spoiled.

Dante, with whom she reverted back to that lonely girl come to live with a distant father, distracted brother and a resented changeling, after her mama's sudden death.

With Dante she would always be her worst self.

Panic skittled over her skin like a line of fire ants crawling up her legs. She needed to marry Dante like she needed a hole in her head. It would be like all the bad decisions she'd ever made steamrolled into one giant boulder that would chase her for the rest of her life.

A hysterical sound released from her mouth.

"Alisha?"

She brought her gaze to his, stood up from the booth, picked up her clutch and turned. "You've gone mad."

"Alisha, wait."

Nope.

She didn't want to hear more. If she did, he would rope her into it.

As a master strategist, he wouldn't have sought her out across the world, wouldn't have approached her if he hadn't already figured out a way to make her agree. And she needed to flee before that happened. Before their lives were even more tangled. Before she betrayed herself in the worst way possible.

Dear God, when it came to him, all she had left was her pride.

"Alisha, stop!" His arm shot out just as Ali got ready to sprint across the restaurant if necessary.

Long fingers roped around her wrist and because of her desperate forward momentum, her foot jerked to the side. Pain shot up through her ankle and she fell back against him.

The breath punched out of her as he anchored her by throwing his arm around her midriff.

Unstoppable force meets immovable object...

"What happens when they crash, Alisha? Who gets destroyed?"

The world stopped tilting at that silky whisper as she realized she'd spoken out loud. And yet, the explosion his touch evoked continued to rock through her body.

The scent of him was all over her skin, filling each pore, drowning her in masculine heat. His legs were thrown wide, the tensile power of his thighs just grazing the back of hers, his chest pushed up tight against her back. Her chest expanded as she tried to stop the panic. On the exhale, the underside of her breasts fell against his steely arm. A soft hiss of warm air bathed her neck, making it a thousand times worse. Or was that pleasure skittering across her skin?

An onslaught of sensations poured through her, her skin prickling tight, and yet, a strange lethargy crawled through her limbs. She wanted to lean into him completely, until her bottom was resting against his hips. She wanted to feel him from chest to toe against her back, she wanted to rub herself against that hard body until he was as mindlessly aroused as her. Until that iron will of his snapped like a thinly stretched rubber band.

As if he could guess the direction of her thoughts, his fingers tightened around her hip, digging into her slightly to keep her still; to keep her from leaning back and learning his body's reaction to her.

Because, really, in what universe did she imagine Dante would want her back with this same madness?

She groaned—a feral, desperate sound. Why was it that everything she did came back to taunt her a thousand times worse?

"Because you don't think before you do," came the voice at her ear. Ah…perfect! Of course, she'd said that out loud too. "You're impulsive, brash and if I hadn't caught you, you would have fallen flat on your face."

"Kissing the floor sounds like a better alternative," she said, her words throaty and whispery.

"Will you sit down and listen if I let you go?"

As if operating on an instinct that defied rationality, her fingers clenched over his wrist.

She opened her eyes and swallowed hard. Since he'd undone his cuffs earlier, her palm rested against a hair-roughened wrist. She rubbed the skin—the rough texture, the plump veins on the back of his hand—the startlingly sensual contrast between her and him inviting her along further and further.

It was the sharp inhale followed by another curse that pulled her out of the fog.

Her chin flopped down to her chest. "No. I don't want to hear anything you say. I don't want to be near... you in this moment, much less in the future."

The vulnerability she fought every waking minute, the longing for a deeper connection in her past, with anyone related to her past, pervaded her in his presence.

This was what would happen if she agreed: every look, every touch would wind her up; lines between want and hate, reality and fantasy would blur...until she attacked him—claws and all—just to keep herself tethered, to keep herself together. Or until she gave in to this inexplicable yearning she had felt for him for so long.

The stiffness of her posture drained away and she leaned back against his chest. She let herself be weak and vulnerable for five seconds.

Both of his arms wound around her. He held her gently, tenderly and that...that was more than Ali could bear. That uncharacteristic moment between them, the mere thought that he could pity her uncontrollable attraction to him, snapped her out of it.

She wriggled in his embrace and he instantly let her go.

Pushing her hair back, she fought for composure. The glass of cold water down her throat was a much needed burst of reality. When he sat down, when she had her wits together again, she looked back at him. "Tell me why."

"Vikram's been declared legally dead."

Gray gaze drinking her in, he paused. Ali looked away.

That he knew what her brother meant to her, that he had seen firsthand that night her grief, her regrets, it was something she couldn't erase. This nebulous connection between her and Dante—despite the knotted history of it—was the only thing she had of her past. And however far she ran, it seemed she would never be free of it. "And?"

"Your uncle will contest for his voting shares and might win. I'd like to crush his little rebellion with as few resources and as little time as possible. I have a huge merger coming up with a Japanese manufacturing company that I need all my energies focused on. Thousands of jobs and thousands more livelihoods depend on that merger. He's well-known for his ability to create PR damage."

So that was what he'd been counting on—that Ali's loathing of her uncle was greater than her combined loathing of her papa and Dante.

Her uncle had driven a wedge between her parents, though Ali knew it had been her father that had finally broken them apart.

Her father's ambition. Her father's unending hunger for success.

Just like the breathtakingly stunning man sitting across from her.

"I never realized what a true legacy you are of papa. Not Vicky, but you."

"Vicky always blazed his own path."

She nodded, the depth of her grief for her brother a hole in her chest. At least that was one thing she couldn't blame Dante for. Her brother had been a technical genius with no interest in his papa's company.

"If I marry you, I can transfer my shares to you and the eventual fate of Vicky's shares won't really matter. You can continue to be the master of Matta Steel." Even she couldn't dispute the trailblazing new heights that Dante had taken the company to since her father's death.

"*Si.* Your vow not to touch a penny of your father's fortune will not be broken since the voting shares are yours through your mother. Monetarily, they don't have much value, since they can't be sold off, or transferred to anyone outside marriage. So this is a good deal for you."

He had a well-rehearsed answer for every contentious point she could raise. "What do I get in return?"

"Money to throw into the drain that is the Lonely Hearts Foundation."

She refused to bite into that judgmental tone. "As much as I want?"

"A pre-agreed upon amount, *si.*"

"I want a check—from your own personal fortune," she added, determined to wring every drop of blood from him, "for that amount. If I agree."

There was a glint in his eye and a slick smile around his mouth, arrogant confidence dripping from every pore. *"Bene."* A regal nod to her request. "From my personal fortune, *si*?"

And whatever she demanded would be a drop in the ocean for him.

"We can't annul or end the marriage for three years or they will revert back to you. We'll both sign a pre-nup. At the end of the three years, a substantial amount of money will be settled on you."

"I don't want a settlement, I don't want a penny from you. And I won't—"

"Don't be foolish, Alisha. Throwing away your in-heritance when you were eighteen was one thing but—"

"—under any circumstances sign a prenup," she delivered that with all the satisfaction of a well-placed right hook.

Shock etched onto those arrogantly handsome features.

It wasn't wise tweaking the tail of a tiger, especially when he was so royally wound up. But if she expected an outburst, a small glimpse of his infamous Sicilian temper that cowed all his employees, Ali was disappointed. Only a small tic in that granite jaw even betrayed how…thrown he was by her coup de grâce. Since he had dropped the whole thing on her with the sensitivity of a bulldozer, she'd pulled that out pretty fast based on that instinct she'd honed for years to annoy the heck out of him.

But now she realized how much she needed that illusion of control over…this. The only way she could keep the balance in this relationship of theirs was not to give him everything he wanted.

"Why not sign the prenup? All it does is give you money I know you won't touch."

She smiled, thoroughly enjoying herself. "Is that praise I hear for my principles?"

"If you think mucking around through life, running from your own shadow is principled, all power to you. I call it a juvenile need for petty revenge you've yet to outgrow. And I keep waiting for you to wake up from this…protracted dream of yours, for the thud of reality to hit you.

"I know spoiled princesses like you like the back of my hand. There will be a day when you'll crawl back to the luxury of your old life with your tail tucked between your legs. Because, really, what have you achieved in the last six years, except to sell off your mama's jewelry piece by priceless piece?

"Sign the prenup. When that day comes, you'll be thankful to me for giving you that option to fall back on."

Wow, he wasn't pulling his punches. Somehow, Ali kept her smile from sliding off her face.

His matter-of-fact assessment of her stung more than it should. She'd seen that same lack of respect, that same exaggerated patience in her father's eyes on the eve of her eighteenth birthday.

As if dressing like a skank and making out with a former junkie rock star in front of their esteemed guests was all he had expected of Ali. And before she could change his impression of her, before she could apologize for her share of mistakes, he'd been lost to her.

But, if it was the last thing she did, she resolved to change Dante's opinion of her.

Not because she wanted his approval—okay, she did, in some throwback to her angsty, unwise, earlier self— but because she wanted to prove him wrong. She needed to bring that arrogance down more than a peg or two. Really, she was doing a public service on behalf of all the women of the planet.

She needed to find some kind of closure for all the painful history between them. She longed for the day when she could look him in the eye and feel nothing.

No attraction. No wistful ache. No emotional connection whatsoever.

"No. No prenup. Let's not forget I'm doing you a favor. I know you're used to people bending over backward for you but I—"

Dark heat flared in his gray eyes. "Do you really want to threaten me about what I can or can't do with you, Alisha?"

Ali jerked back, the temperature cocoon soaring from arctic cold to desert hot within seconds. Red-hot images of herself doing his bidding, forbidden images of their limbs tangling…the heat between them was a near tangible thing in the air.

Did that mean he felt it too?

Walk away now, Ali. Walk away before you're far too tempted to resist.

But the thought of being able to save the charity that meant so much to her mother, the thought of returning to London, the thoughts of being grounded for a while, the thought of proving to Dante that she wasn't a car crash in the making won out. "I want your word that this agreement is only on paper. That you won't use it to manage me, to manage my life in any way."

His fingers roped over her wrists like a gnarly vine. That accent slipped in through his soft words. "Do not think to play those silly games with me that you did with your father, Alisha. I will not let you drag my name through mud like you did his. No splashing yourself all over the media with some ex-junkie. No sneaking out behind my back with another man. At least not when you're in London."

"If you're not careful with your threats, you're going to sound like a real fiancé, Dante." Whatever his conditions, she knew she'd have no problem keeping them. Like she'd already told him, her days of doing things to wind him up were over.

But she wouldn't let Dante have all the power in this relationship. "Let me get this straight. If I give up men for three years, will you do the same? Will you be celibate for three years?"

"I won't be the reason my name or this agreement of ours gets dragged through the mud."

"That's not really answering the question."

"My name, my reputation…they mean everything to me, Alisha. I built them brick by brick from nothing. Away from the shadow of my father's crime.

"I created a new life from the ground up. I built my fortune, I made my reputation anew after everything I had was destroyed in a matter of days." Ali shivered at the dark intensity of his words, the specter of his past almost a live thing between them. With his ruthless ambition coating every word, it was easy to forget what had brought Dante to her father at all. What had built him up to be this man she saw now.

"You put one toe out of line during any of this and your precious charity won't get a penny."

CHAPTER FOUR

SHE WAS LATE.

Of course she was. It was his own fault for assuming Alisha could ever be a headache-free zone for him. What he should have done was show up at the dingy flat she lived in, insist she pack up and drag her to the airstrip.

Instead, he'd given them both a few days to gain perspective. To make sure he could think, away from the distraction of her...presence. Of her outrageous demands. Like the demand that he forward a sum of ten thousand pounds as the first payment.

Already, his lawyer was freaking out at the massive risk Dante was leaving himself open to by marrying her without a prenup.

And that was before the man found out what a firecracker Alisha was.

But for all the threats and warnings his lawyer had screamed over the transatlantic call, Dante couldn't see her using this marriage to fleece him, to build her own fortune. He couldn't see her dragging him into some kind of court battle—but threatening to sully his reputation in a rage, yes.

That he was more than ready for. In fact, the idea of sparring with Alisha now, the very idea of going toe-to-toe with her sent a shiver of excitement through him. *Cristo*, his life was truly devoid of fun if a battle with Alisha filled him with this much anticipation.

He'd called it her protracted, rebellious phase—he had thought her a spoiled princess but he was beginning to question that. He had had his chauffeur drive him past her flat, he'd seen where she waitressed sometimes. And she'd lived like that for more than five years.

Common sense pointed out that she wasn't going to come after his fortune. Or Matta Steel.

The realization both calmed and unnerved him. Because, for the first time in his life, he had a feeling that reassurance came mostly from a place of emotion, despite the logic of it too. But he was determined to keep control of the situation.

If she thought he was handing over that amount of money without asking questions…if she thought he'd let her play him, play fast and loose in London, if she thought being his wife in name was just the latest weapon she could use against him…

It was time to reacquaint her with her adversary and set the ground rules for this…agreement between them. He refused to call it a marriage, refused to give his suddenly overdeveloped sense of guilt any more material to chew on.

Which was why he was waiting in Bangkok to accompany her back to London in his private jet rather than have his security bring her. He was also determined to accompany her because her return to London would definitely be commented on by the press, and once they announced that they had married, even their planned civil union without pomp and fanfare would still occupy the news cycle for a couple of weeks at least.

Thanks to his father's notoriety during his life and the spectacle of his suicide during his incarceration alongside Dante's swift rise through the ranks of Matta Steel to the position of CEO, there was plenty for the media to chew on. They were always ready to find some chink in his personality, some weak link in his makeup to crow that he was his criminal father's flawed son.

Sometimes they did get their hands on a juicy story from a woman he'd dumped—for the simple reason that she wanted more from the relationship and he didn't. Dante didn't care a hoot about a tabloid feature.

But this…agreement with Alisha would be no small step in the eyes of the media and the world. As such he needed to make her understand the importance of her behavior in the coming months.

The stubborn defiance in her eyes, the stark silence she'd subjected him to through the drive back to her flat hadn't been lost on him.

Alisha didn't respond well to threats.

He remembered the two-day disappearance she'd engineered when, on Neel's instructions, Dante had tried to enroll her in a boarding school in Paris a couple of months after she'd first come to live with her father.

Fighting the near constant hum of his attraction to her had briefly made him forget that.

This was a business deal and he couldn't antagonize Alisha any more than he would lose his temper with a new business partner. There had to be a way to get her to behave, to cooperate without letting the full force of his contempt for her to shine through.

The one thing he knew for certain was that he couldn't punish her for his own attraction to her, for his lack of self-control. And as much as his mind and body were bent on reminding him that she had fancied him once, he refused to go down that road.

No.

After the first hour, he stepped out of his car. The unusually heavy wind roared in his ears and he pushed up his sunglasses even though the sun had yet to make an appearance on the chilly late September morning.

Patience had never been his strong point. And yet he had a feeling that it would be stretched to the limit in the near future. A few months with Alisha was bound to turn him mental in his thirties.

He continued to wait and was just about to call her when a caravan of cars—really, a who's who of colorful vintage cars in different stages of deterioration—pulled up on the long, curving road that led to the airstrip.

Laughter bubbled out of his chest. He sensed his security team giving him sidelong, concerned looks. Well, no one ever made him laugh like Alisha did. Neither had a woman tested his control, or called forth some of his base instincts with a single smile like she did.

How fitting that the drama queen arrived in a ramshackle entourage of her own.

The caravan came to a stop with a lot of screeching noise that confirmed his suspicion that all three cars were on their last legs. But what crawled out of the cars was even more shocking. A surprising number of people clambered out of those small cars, a torrent of English and Thai flowing around. Car trunks were opened and suitcases and bags in different colors and makes pulled out.

Emerging from the third car, dressed again in short shorts that should have been banned, and a chunky sweater that fell to her thighs, almost covering the shorts, was Alisha. Loose and oversize, it fell off one shoulder almost to her bicep, leaving a hot-pink bra strap exposed.

And there was that same black camera bag—heavy from the looks of how the wide strap pulled over one shoulder and between her breasts.

Hair in that messy bun. No jewelry. Combat style boots on her feet.

No makeup that he could see. In fact, in the gray morning light, she looked freshly scrubbed, innocent and so excruciatingly lovely that he felt a tug low in his belly as surely as the sun peeking through the clouds.

Her wide smiles and husky laughter made her eyes twinkle. She stood among the loud group like sun shining on a vast field of sunflowers, every face turned toward her with genuine affection, long limbs grabbing her, hugging her, men and women kissing her cheeks. A sense of disbelief went through him as he spied a sheen of tears as she hugged the man called Mak.

And then she met his eyes.

Current arced between them even across the distance. As one, the group turned their gazes on him. Instead of surprise or curiosity, there was a certain knowledge in the looks leveled at him, knowledge about him. A certain warning in the looks, a subtle crowding around her, as if Alisha had imparted her opinion of him.

Out of the blue, for the first time in their shared history, he wondered what Alisha thought of him. What was behind all that…resentment of him? Did she still believe he'd stolen her legacy?

That hum began again under his skin as she pushed away from the crowd.

His breath suspended in his throat as the subtle scent of her skin teased him. He felt an overwhelming urge to bury his nose in her throat; to see that gorgeous, open smile leveled at him.

"Do you have the money ready?"

"All ten thousand pounds, *si*," he responded, a hint of warning in his tone.

She pulled out a slip from the back pocket of her shorts, the action thrusting her breasts up. He gaped like a teenager until she said, "Please have it transferred to this bank account."

He looked at the slip of paper with a routing number and an account number and raised his brows. "Whose account is it?"

"Kiki and Mak's joint account." She sighed at his silence. "You can't place conditions on how I use the money. No micromanaging my life."

"You're not doing this to piss me off, are you?"

She rolled her eyes. "No. As much as our shared history gives you reason to believe that, I'm not."

He took a step toward her. "Are they blackmailing

you? Whatever it is, I'll take care of it. What was it, Alisha? Drugs they hooked you into? Naked pictures?"

"What do you mean, naked pictures?"

Her shock was so genuine that it took Dante a couple of seconds to speak. "Who do you think took care of that junkie rock star before he could sell your pics to every tabloid magazine?"

A frown tied her brow, her gaze staring at him unseeingly. "Richard threatened to sell naked pictures of me? Did you see them?"

"Of course I didn't look at your pictures," he snapped. "He gave us enough proof to show it was you."

He pushed a hand through his hair, the very prospect of that idiot taking advantage of a young Ali turning him inside out even now. It was the one time in his adult life that Dante had lost his temper and given in to the urge to punch the man's pretty face.

Vikram had had to restrain him physically.

"So did you pay him?" Ali asked softly.

"I don't respond well to threats, just like you. He gave me the flash drive with the pics on it and I smashed it with a paperweight."

She laughed, the sound full of a caustic bitterness. "Wow, you really don't think much of me, do you?" Her mouth trembled. "Mak and Kiki are the last people who would blackmail anyone. For the first year, when I moved here, I didn't pay for anything. Board or food. Whatever I pay them, believe me, it's very little in return for what they did for me."

Would the woman never develop a sense of self-preservation? "It's not a hardship to be kind to an heiress, Alisha. A payoff is usually expected at some point."

Hurt painted her small smile, her eyes widening, even as she bravely tilted her chin.

He had hurt her. The realization sat tightly on his chest.

"They don't know who I am, Dante. When you showed up at the restaurant a week ago, it was the first time I told either of them who I was."

"Alisha, I don't—"

"And if you say some stupid thing like I haven't earned it to give it away, believe me I did. Mama earned each and every one of those voting shares. She lost Papa to the blasted company. And all she got were those in return. So, yes, she paid for them. And y'know what? I paid for them too because I should've grown up with my father and brother and Mama in the same house. I shouldn't have had to wonder why Papa barely visited me. Vicky shouldn't have had to wonder how Mama could have so easily given him up. I shouldn't have had to wonder why it took Mama's death for him to be in my life.

"I shouldn't have to wonder what I lacked that meant he chose…" Her chest rose and fell, a haunting light in her eyes. "I paid for those shares, Dante. And I want some good to come out of what I'm signing up for with you. Something to ground me when you drive me up the wall over the next few months. That money will be a nice deposit for the business Mak and Kiki want to begin." She swallowed and met his gaze. "They welcomed me with open arms when I desperately needed friends, when I needed to be loved."

The vulnerability in her words struck him like a punch to his solar plexus, bringing in its wake a cold helplessness.

I'm not that impulsive, destructive Ali anymore.

Her words from a week ago haunted Dante as he watched her climb the steps to the aircraft. Maybe she wasn't that same old Alisha anymore. But as far as he knew, people didn't really change.

A reckless Alisha wouldn't have visited London three times and tried to patch up her mother's favorite charity.

A spoiled Alisha wouldn't have lived in anonymity when she could have simply used her father's name to live in luxury.

So maybe he hadn't known Alisha at all.

Maybe he didn't know the woman he was marrying after all.

CHAPTER FIVE

ALI STARED MINDLESSLY as she stepped onto the flight and elegant luxury met her eyes. Every moment she spent with Dante, the past relentlessly pulled at her. Along with all the moronic decisions she'd made in anger, in hurt, coming back to take a chunk out of her ass.

From the moment she'd stepped out of the car, she'd been aware of his eyes on her every second. His silent scrutiny, the way his gaze devoured her expression made her skin feel stretched tight. Any hope she had indulged that that pulse of attraction at the restaurant was just a heightened reaction because she was seeing him for the first time in six years died a quick death.

Even with her friends surrounding her—she still couldn't believe how many of them had showed up—she'd been aware of him.

It was as if, overnight, she'd developed an extra sense. A sixth sense that evolved to keep her in tune with Dante's every move, his every look, his every breath. And now they had twelve hours of flight in the enclosed space together, and the fact that the interior of the aircraft was much more expansive and luxurious than a commercial flight made no difference whatsoever.

Feeling hot and agitated, she tugged at the hem of her sweater and pulled it up in one quick move.

Like her, Dante also shed his jacket with a flick of those powerful shoulders.

Trying to look away was like the earth trying to pull out from its orbit around the sun. The cabin shrunk around them, and her breaths became shallow. Even before takeoff, oxygen was in short supply.

Instead of his formal attire, which was second skin to him, today he wore a sky blue polo T-shirt that made his gray eyes pop.

If virility needed a picture in the dictionary, Dante would be perfect.

For virility see Dante Vittori.

Just the sight of his biceps and thick arms with a dusting of dark hair was enough to send her belly swooping. The blue denim clung to his tapering hips and powerful thighs. Ali sighed and pulled in a long breath. God, this was going to be a long flight. She couldn't take this much of him—the proximity, the constant awareness, the constant tugging in her belly urging her to look at him, to breathe him in.

And she craved more.

It wasn't just the physical attraction.

When she'd first moved in with her father after her mama's death, Dante had made quite the impression on her.

He'd been serious, brooding, off the charts handsome, and the worst of all: so close to her father—something she'd desperately needed but hadn't had. Her papa's eyes had been so full of pride for his protégé's achievements, his single-minded focus, his ambition.

At thirteen, she'd been hormonal, lost and he had been a hero, the golden son who had gotten everything she'd coveted. The one man who seemed more confident, more powerful, more handsome than any she'd known. She'd left London five years before because she'd been lost, grieving, sick of the imbalance in the dynamic between them.

Yet, it seemed nothing had changed.

Would he always be like this to her—this magnetic, confident embodiment of the perfect man? She looked up and found his gaze on her. Clearly disapproving. "What? Why are you giving me the stink eye?"

"The stink eye? What are we, six?"

"I could be six. You're what…a hundred and thirty now?"

The soft material of his T-shirt stretched taut across his wide chest and hard abdomen, mocking her words. "I'm old because I don't engage in childish behavior and language? Because I show up on time?"

"No, you're old because you…" Her words veered off as he walked closer, the very air filled with his dark masculinity. "You were probably born old with no sense of humor and an exaggerated sense of your own importance."

He raised a brow.

Heat rushed up her neck. "Okay, fine. I was two hours late, but I'm not really sorry. I told you I couldn't make a seven a.m. flight. You went ahead anyway. We planned Kiki's birthday party four months ago and it had to be this morning."

"You couldn't have had it last night?"

"She works nights. So it's your own fault if you waited for two hours. I told you, Dante, this whole thing…isn't going to be all by your rules. You're going to have to treat me like an adult."

"*Bene.* As long as you conduct yourself like one."

"Fine."

"Now that we have gotten that out of the way, I have some things I would like to discuss."

Ali folded her arms and tilted her chin up. "*Fine.* But first you have to feed me. I haven't had anything to eat since yesterday afternoon."

"No wonder you look like a bag of bones."

"I'm sorry I'm not curvy enough to fit your standards."

He sighed.

Ali scrunched her nose. "Hunger makes me cranky."

His mouth twitched. "Is that an apology?"

"Of sorts."

He nodded and like magic, the flight attendant arrived with a tray.

Ali dug into the bowl of creamy penne pasta with a delicate white wine sauce. The soft clink of the silver utensils filled the silence, which had an almost comfortable quality to it. It was only when he looked at her, as if he meant to see into her soul, as if she was endlessly fascinating, that she got flustered. Great, all she had to do to keep her sanity was avoid looking at him. "Okay, talk."

Dante seated himself in the opposite seat from Alisha and stretched his legs the other way. He'd stared earlier, his thoughts going in an altogether wicked direction when she'd removed the sweater and it had made her nervous. Which in turn had made her flippant. How was it that it had taken him that long to figure out that that was Alisha's default when she was unsure of herself?

"A team is airing out Matta Mansion as we speak. It's quite a drive from my flat in central London but it should work. You'll make it your home base for the near future and I can visit you there. There'll be a certain amount of media coverage on this so Matta Mansion will provide the perfect cover. My PR team's drafting a statement to announce our engagement."

"I don't want to live there."

Dante gritted his teeth, determined not to lose his temper. "Alisha, you just promised that you wouldn't fight me on every single thing."

"And you said you wouldn't railroad me. I can't…" Distress filled her eyes and his retort died on his lips. "I won't go back there. Not without Vikram and Papa. Not to an empty house…" She looked away, her profile lovely as she swallowed.

Dante sat back in his seat, fighting the urge to pull her into his arms and soothe her. *Cristo*, living with Alisha would be like riding a never-ending roller coaster.

One moment he wanted to throttle her, one moment kiss her senseless and the next hold her tight.

He wanted her where he could keep an eye on her. Especially because of the media storm she didn't understand would hit them. "That only leaves my flat."

The devilish imp was back in her eyes when she turned to him. "I never thought I'd see the ruthless Dante Vittori scared."

Again, that overwhelming sense of relief poured through him. The vulnerability in her eyes sometimes made him feel like that adolescent youth again—powerless and all too aware of his own needs. And in its wake came the most overwhelming urge to hold her and kiss her until it was gone from her eyes.

Pure lust, he could handle. This…dangerous urge to play her hero—no!

"Scared?" he asked.

"The idea of me in your flat terrifies you to your hardened soul."

He laughed and the sound of it was a shock to his own ears. She dug her teeth into her lower lip, but couldn't quite arrest her smile either. "Fine, the flat it is. But—"

"I'll respect the rules of your domain. I'll control the urge to have orgies every night. I'll be mindful of your pristine reputation and the shadow I could cast over it as your wife. How was that?"

He was still smiling. "That sounds like you drafted it."

"All night," she retorted, the irreverent minx. "Anything I missed?"

He shook his head, all the threats and conditions he meant to impose on her disappearing from his mind. She was a live wire, he didn't forget that for one second. Nor could he think. Because of the manifesto she'd read him, his ordered and peaceful life would remain that. And yet, he couldn't muster a sense of dread over it. He couldn't bring the words to his lips to kill that wide smile. He couldn't contain the little flare of excitement in his blood every time she leveled those eyes on him, every time she fought with him, every time she looked away but not before he saw the interest she couldn't hide in her eyes.

This was a dangerous high he was chasing, and *Dios mio*, where was his sense of self-preservation? So when he said, "What about you?" his voice was harsh.

She raised a brow. "What about me?"

"Any demands or expectations?"

"Not really. I'm…excited to put your money into the charity. I have some contacts I would like to network—"

"For what?"

"For my photography," she said, her smile dimming. "I'm going to see if I can sell them in the market for a penny a piece." Shift to sarcasm. It was like watching a panorama of emotions. "Oh, I also need a studio—a darkroom essentially." Back to a practical survival instinct he couldn't help but admire. "All in all, I'm looking forward to being back in London."

"You develop your own prints?"

"Yes."

"I'll arrange it."

"Thank you. Between the charity and the darkroom,

you won't see me. Your perfectly ordered life will remain just the same."

Put like that, she sounded so sensible that Dante wanted to believe it. He not only had to believe it, he had to keep it like that. There was no feasible route his fascination with her could take.

No other outcome was possible between them. No other.

Ali had no idea if it was the unusually long-lasting peace on the flight or being back in London under the same roof, but the moment Dante showed her into the guest room, she made the connection she'd missed earlier.

What he'd said had been eating at her.

Richard had tried to blackmail Dante for those pics...great judgment call, Ali!

She finished her shower in a hurry, and pulled on the first pair of panties, shorts and T-shirt she could find in her bag. Hair wet and dripping down her back, she barefooted it to Dante's door.

He opened on the first knock, his hands pulling his T-shirt from those jeans. The slab of abdominal muscles she spied before she jerked her gaze to his almost made her forget why she sought him out. Almost.

She stepped back as he closed the door behind him.

"Alisha? What is it?"

"You said 'us'. You told Papa about the pictures Richard claimed he had, didn't you?"

It had been exactly around that time that she'd been summoned into her father's study and while her father had sat silently in the corner—his disappointment a noxious cloud in the air—Dante had informed her that she wouldn't be going away as apprentice to a world-renowned photographer as planned. Or at least, the exorbitant fee she'd needed to pay wouldn't be coming from her father's bank account.

Vikram, as usual, had been absent, working in his lab, and her father had refused to talk to her that evening, even as she'd pleaded with him to rethink his decision. That was the last time she'd talked to her father.

Dread coursed through her that she was once again locking herself in that bubble with Dante, her mind and body constantly battling it out.

Dante stilled. "What?"

"That's why he…cut me off. Refused to pay the fee for that apprenticeship. You told him and I lost a chance at the one thing I wanted to do most in the world. Being accepted into that program…it was the one thing that got me through so much. Through Mama's death, through being thrust into living with you three strangers…and because of you, I lost the opportunity to learn, to see if I could follow my passion.

"Did you hate me so much, Dante? Yes, I made impulsive, rash decisions, but you know what the worst part of it was? Papa died thinking I was determined to shame him in front of the world."

Tears filled her eyes. She swiped at them angrily. Regrets were useless. The past was done.

His fingers on her arm turned her, his grip a vise. Ali couldn't look up, everything in her cringing that he saw her like this. The last thing she wanted was his pity.

"Alisha, look at me. Alisha!" His growl filled the space between them. "I didn't tell Neel, okay? I just dealt with Richard. Vicky told your father."

She blinked. "What? Why?"

"Vicky loved you and…he was worried for you. He felt guilty for neglecting you for so long, for being pre-occupied with his lab. He convinced Neel that separating you from the heiress label would cut off all the hangers-on and leeches. Maybe ground you a little. Give you a chance to see the reality of your friends. I…"

"What, Dante?"

"I tried to persuade Neel not to do that."

"I don't believe you."

He flinched. Just a tremble of that upper lip, but it was there. "I told you, I'm not your enemy. You reminded me of someone I despised for so long. You were spoiled and immature and rebellious, but I didn't hate you.

"I knew photography meant everything to you, how *not*…miserable or angry or rebellious you were when you walked around clicking away on that old camera. I tried to convince Neel that he could pay the fee and still cut you off from the rest of your trust fund. He wouldn't listen. I think he felt you'd pushed him too far that time."

Ali nodded, her chest so tight that it took all her wits to keep breathing. Dante had supported her. Dante had intervened on her behalf. "That's funny, isn't it? All the tantrums I threw for his attention, all the really bad decisions I made because I was so lost…and he punished me for the one thing I didn't do by taking away the most important thing to me. I beat myself up every day that I didn't take the chance to get to know him, that I ruined our relationship. But he didn't even try to get to know me."

"I think you reminded him too much of Shanti. He never got over the fact that she left him."

"That's not my fault. I was a child, and so was Vicky."

Something dawned in those jet-black eyes. He ran a hand over his face, exhaling a long breath. "He was a good man, but not perfect." Suddenly, his head jerked up, his gaze pinning Ali to the spot. "What do you mean he punished you for something you didn't do?"

"I don't know what Richard showed you but I never posed for any pictures naked. And even if I had, even if I had made bad choices, I didn't deserve to be punished by Papa and Vicky and you for it. You three had each other. Who did I have?"

He jerked back, a whiteness around his mouth.

She'd shocked him—with the truth or with her tears, she had no idea. But for once, it didn't feel good to shock Dante. How could she think anything but hurt and destruction could result from this stupid agreement?

Ali was almost out of his sight when she stilled.

I knew photography meant everything to you.

No, no, no.

He couldn't have, could he?

She didn't want to ask, she didn't want to know. But the question would eat her up.

Dante reached for her, his fingers drawing circles over her wrist. "Alisha, what?"

Just weeks after that scene with her father, mere days after she'd moved out of the mansion once and for all, she'd received the camera. One of the costliest professional cameras on the market—almost forty thousand pounds even five years ago, it had arrived by a special courier.

With no message.

It was not the most expensive thing she'd received in her life, thanks to her father's birthday gifts every year. But it had been the most thoughtful present anyone had bought her, the present that had brought her more joy, more peace than anything else.

She'd simply assumed at the time that it was Vicky's gift. She'd even texted him thanks but had never received anything back. She'd attributed it to her brother's usual neglect of any communications.

"My Nikon XFD45…"

He didn't quite shy away his gaze from her but Dante released her instantly. "There's nothing to be achieved by raking over the past." He patted the pad of his thumb under her eyes, a quick, feathery stroke, something dark flashing in his eyes. "You're tired. Go to bed."

Ali pushed into his personal space, heart racing. "Dante, who bought that camera for me? Who sent it to me?" And when he opened his mouth to blurt out some nontruth, she covered his mouth with her palm. "Please, Dante, the truth."

He pushed away her hand from his mouth. His nostrils flared, emotion glinting in his eyes.

"I did. I saw how you cried that night. I argued with Neel to no avail. And when I went to your bedroom and found it empty, I knew you weren't coming back. Days later, it wouldn't leave me alone so I ordered the camera."

Words of gratitude hovered on her lips. She'd always viewed him as the enemy, had hated him on principle, but this one gift...it didn't negate all the barbed history they shared. And yet, suddenly, Ali felt like the ground had been stolen from under her.

"Why didn't you—?"

"I felt guilty that evening. Powerless to right what I thought was a needlessly harsh action against you." His mouth took on that forbidding slant she knew well. "Of course, you pushed and pushed and pushed me... yes. But after I realized you were..." It was as if he couldn't put into words what he felt. "Buying that camera for you relieved my guilt. Don't read too much into it, Alisha."

For once, Ali didn't balk at his dismissal. She was more than ready to leave behind the cutting awareness of being near him, of the seesaw of her own emotions.

But as she dried her hair and crawled into bed exhausted, her heart refused to believe the perfectly rational explanation Dante offered.

He'd asked Papa not to take away the photography program from her.

He'd checked on her, even if it had been out of guilt.

He'd bought her that camera, knowing how much it would mean to her.

Maybe he had cared about her a little. Maybe Dante wasn't...

That sent a sharp spike of fear through her rambling mind, had her sitting up in the bed even as her eyes burned for sleep.

This whole idea of a platonic marriage between them, her very sanity, hinged on the fact that Dante was an unfeeling, ambitious man.

If that fell apart, what else was left to protect her heart from the intimacy of the next few years, from her foolish attraction, from her own endlessly naive heart?

CHAPTER SIX

THUD. THUD.

"Alisha?"

Thud. Soft *thud.* Followed by a curse in Italian.

"Alisha, fifteen minutes or I break down this door."

They were tight, softly spoken words, and yet filled with that controlled fury they made Ali jump. She stepped out of the hot shower that she'd been standing under for far too long. She shivered and grabbed two towels—one for her hair, and one for her body. Her cell phone chirped and she glanced at the time and grimaced.

She glanced at the date and grimaced a little more. Any more grimacing and her face was going to be permanently frozen into a...grimace.

Today was the morning of her wedding. To Dante.

She was marrying Dante today.

Or Dante was marrying her?

Ten days of repeating that to herself hadn't made it any easier to face today.

She hurriedly toweled down her body, threw on panties, tugged on denim shorts and a loose T-shirt, just as the knock came again.

Toweling her hair with one hand, she opened the door. Dante pushed inside.

The towel fell from her hands while her heart thudded against her rib cage. Ali rubbed at her chest and stared at him, a prickle of heat flushing all over her and pooling between her legs.

She groaned and closed her eyes. But nothing could erase the sight of him from her mind. Strikingly handsome didn't do him justice at all.

Black jacket that defined his powerful shoulders; white dress shirt that stretched against his broad chest; black pants that molded to his powerful thighs; jet-black hair slicked back, gleaming with wetness. A smooth shave of that sharp, defined jawline that she wanted to run her tongue along; dark eyes—penetrating and gorgeous, glimmering with interest and intensity.

He was too much.

This was far too much for anyone to bear. If she'd known all her bad decisions and all the pain she'd caused her papa and her brother and Dante could come back to her in this form… Karma was indeed a bitch.

Ten days of being back in London, ten days of seeing Dante every morning, impeccably dressed in a three-piece suit—sometimes he was ready to leave for the day when she was getting ready to crawl into bed after hours spent in the darkroom—had taken a toll on her mental health.

It was too much Dante to stomach on any given day.

Furthermore, he'd been determined to oversee a wardrobe upgrade for her because no, he still didn't trust her not to play some cheap trick to embarrass him.

They'd also been forced together while he explained in detail the legalities of transferring her voting shares that he insisted she understand, and because of her ill-thought-out idea of coming to him with some financial questions regarding her mom's charity—the only time she sought him of her own accord. Yes, they had spent far too much time, far too close to each other.

In the blink of an eye, she could now recall a hundred different expressions he wore.

With one breath, she could remember the scent of him.

At the drop of a hat, in the middle of the night or day, whether she was at the Lonely Hearts HQ or in her darkroom, she could conjure the curve of his mouth when he smiled, the laconic glint in his eyes when she was flippant, the way his nostrils flared and his jaw tightened when she annoyed him.

It was as though her mind was happily compiling a database of Dante-related details to draw upon whenever and wherever it wanted.

As a teenager, it had been an inexplicable obsession, a weird love-hate relationship, a mild form of nauseating hero worship. Within a few days of returning to London she'd learned that she knew nothing of the real man beneath the insufferable arrogance and ruthless ambition. It was only after she'd burst the bubble of illusion had she realized the safety there had been in it.

Now she saw a complex and interesting man. She saw that beneath the ruthless ambition, there was integrity and a moral compass that no one could shake. Beneath the rigid discipline and control, there was a man who knew every single employee by name and their family conditions. There was a man who saw more than profit margin, much as he coated it with what he called simple business tactics. This was the man her father had nurtured and loved.

Where had all the animosity she'd nursed and tended to with such care for almost ten years gone? Was she so pathetically deprived for affection that the stupid camera incident had changed the entire dynamic between them?

It was now replaced by an awkwardness filled with anticipation, tension and lot of tongue-tied staring on her behalf. Like now.

She opened her eyes and caught him doing a leisurely perusal of her T-shirt sticking to her still damp body. Her meager breasts looked round and high, her nipples clearly distended with wetness. Jerkily, she tugged the shirt away.

His jaw tightened, that infinitesimal flare of his nostrils freezing her midaction.

He was just as aware of her as she was of him. Was that possible?

His ankles crossed, he was a picture of masculine arrogance and yet there was tension around that mouth, a wave of something radiating from him, filling the air around them.

Awareness pounded into her, stronger and sharper than an IV of caffeine. He did notice her. He wasn't immune to her. He was…attracted to her?

She swayed on her feet and he was instantly there, anchoring her, a warm marble slab to her touch, his heartbeat a thunder under her skin. She snatched her arm away just as he raised his own.

"You're not ready." Gravelly and husky, he sounded unlike himself.

The moment stretched as they stared at each other, the world outside held at bay. Her skin pulsed, her breasts falling up and down as if she were running.

She wanted to reach out again and touch him. She wanted to run her fingers over that defined jawline, press her tongue against the hollow of his throat, unbutton his shirt just a little and slip her fingers inside until she could feel the sparse hair that dotted his chest— she'd snuck a peek when he'd come in from a run one morning. She wanted to check for herself if his heart was thundering like hers was, run her hands down, down, down until she could trace his hard abdomen, down into his trousers until she could see if he was—

The sound of his curse, gritted out with near-violence sent a blast of heat up Ali's chest and cheeks. "I'm ready, okay? Just…" She rubbed a hand over her forehead, lowering her tone to normal. "As ready as I'll ever be for this. So let's get this over with, please."

He pushed a hand through his slicked-back hair, making it flop forward. "What you're wearing is not… appropriate. Only you can make an old T-shirt look like it should come with a red-hot warning."

The words fell from his mouth fast, totally unlike him. By the skin of her teeth, she somehow, somehow, managed to ignore the rough texture of his tone.

"Not this again, please." She pushed her hand through her hair, realizing it was dripping wet. "All we'll do is sign papers in front of two witnesses. The registrar will make us repeat those vows—which I've learned by heart, okay? I'll sign my name, you'll sign yours. *It will be over.* Nothing changes between us. Everything remains the same." It had been her mantra since she'd woken up at five in the morning.

When he stared back at her with infinite patience, she let her anxiety seep into her tone. "Don't make it harder than it has to be, Dante."

"There'll be press waiting outside the registrar's office."

Ali sank back. "What? Who could have leaked it?"

His hands smoothed over his jacket and he almost seemed reluctant to speak. "I invited them."

"Why?"

"Have you seen the headlines since we returned?"

"Yes."

Just as he'd predicted, there was far too much interest in his every move.

The rebel Matta heiress engaged to her father's protégé and confirmed billionaire bachelor Dante Vittori was far too juicy a story. All her previous transgressions had already been dragged into the spotlight again to contrast her record with Dante's pristine reputation.

There was no doubt in anyone's mind that she was the lesser one, the one found wanting in their coupledom.

A half laugh, half bark tore out of her chest as she remembered the headline that had described Dante on an online gossip site that Ali should've known better than to click. Consequently, she'd fallen into the internet hole of Dante's love life over the past ten years.

Models, actresses, there had even been one popular daytime talk show host. When she'd dug herself out of the hole, like everything related to gossip sites on the net, Alisha had felt like a pervy spectator with ringside seats to his love life.

What was worse was that old feeling of inadequacy, the sense of not being good enough, that had plagued her all her adolescent life and driven her to make horrible choices. Really, it was mind-boggling how she could believe she wasn't enough of a woman for a fake marriage to the perfect male specimen that was Dante Vittori.

Fake marriage, people!

"Isn't it bad enough that my reputation precedes me? Bad enough that every stupid online magazine is speculating that you're somehow saving me by marrying me. Old friends are calling me with all kinds of questions."

He frowned. "Why didn't you tell me? Have they been harassing you?"

"Mrs. Puri, our old housekeeper, called the other day and asked me if I was pregnant. And then blessed you in Hindi for two whole minutes for your loyalty and refused to stop giving me tips on how to be a good Indian bride.

"When I pointed out that you were Sicilian, she went off about how Sicilian men, like their Indian counterparts, expect a traditional, biddable wife. She had the gall to tell me that I was lucky to have caught a handsome, loyal man like you despite all my flaws. I wouldn't have been surprised if there'd been smoke coming out of my ears."

Of all the reactions she'd expected from him, it wasn't the hearty laugh that shot out of his mouth. His eyes lit up as if there was a light behind them, and his teeth flashed white in his olive face. Her fingers itched for her camera. She wanted to capture him in that moment forever. Like a hundred other moments. "I adored Mrs. Puri. How is she?"

Ali glared at him even as parts of her down south melted at how gorgeous he looked. How carefree and approachable and affectionate. "She's happy and cozy in Cambridge with the huge pension you settled on her. Why didn't you tell me you did that for all of Mama and Papa's old staff?"

An uncommunicative shrug. "What else did she say?"

He was still smiling and it felt like the sun was peeking through the gloomy October morning.

"I'm glad you think my life is funny. They think you're coming to my rescue. That my life went off the rails again because of something I'd done, and you, for the sake of Papa, are sacrificing your demigod-like virility on the altar of my thoughtless recklessness. I don't want to give them more—"

A feral smile playing around his mouth, he threaded his hand through her hair and tugged her forward. Mouth dry, heart palpitating, Ali went, like a bow flexing in the hands of a master archer. "Sacrificing my demigod-like virility at the altar of your thoughtless recklessness? Only you can come up with such outrageous descriptions."

She licked her lips and his gaze arrested there. "The

legion of your female admirers saddened by our engagement give complete credence to my statement."

He traced his knuckles against her cheek, a thoughtful curiosity in his eyes. It was barely a touch and yet all of her being pulsed beneath that patch of skin. Slowly, he released her hair and the progressive loss of his addictive scent and his warmth made her want to weep.

"Just the idea of our engagement did that. There's no way to stop the press from following this story like rabid dogs when it comes out that we've married so quickly. They will hound me, but I'm used to it. They'll make your life hell. This way, we give them what we want. We control the narrative. A quick statement from us and a couple of orchestrated shots means the story doesn't take off in a hundred different ways."

"I don't want to pretend anything."

"It'll just be a photographer and one journalist from a reputed online website. They won't even be allowed inside where we sign the papers. Dress like you mean it. Turn the world on its head. Think of it as armor, Alisha. Dazzle them so much that they don't wonder the why of this anymore. Surprise them with all the changes you've made."

"The changes I've made?"

"Haven't you made changes? I barely see you during the day and you're at that studio most nights. Be smart about the publicity you'll garner over the next few months. Use this opportunity. Use me."

Her gaze drifted to his broad shoulders. "Use you?" she whispered, a veritable cornucopia of forbidden, erotic messages downloading into her brain for using him.

"Si." An unusual smile curved his lips. "Being my wife will automatically give you unwanted attention. People who want to get to me will clamor for your attention first. Invitations for lavish dinners and charity events will flow. Make connections. Use these people to build up the charity. You can either hide over the next few months or you can use the time to achieve your goals. It all depends on how you choose to look at the situation."

Put like that, it made so much sense to her.

He was right. It was inevitable that his reputation, his high connections would overshadow her life for a long while. So why not make use of it all for a good cause?

A bright energy infused her veins. For the first time in her life, there was someone who understood her, who encouraged her. On an impulse, she threw herself at him. Arms wrapped around his neck, she pressed a hard kiss to his cheek. It lasted only a few seconds, half a minute at the most.

And yet, she couldn't forget the steely cage of his arms around her waist, the rough smoothness of his cheek, or the way everything in her body felt loose and heavy at the same time.

Pulling away, she refused to look at him.

In her wardrobe, she pulled out a cream, knee-length, silk sleeveless dress, one of the classiest creations she'd ever seen.

The dress slithered over her skin with a soft whisper. But she couldn't get the back zipper all the way. Fake it 'til you mean it. That was what she was going to do. With the world and with Dante.

Face frozen into an unaffected smile, she walked back out and presented her back to him. "Zip me up."

An eon seemed to pass before he tugged the zipper up, and another eternity when the pads of his fingers lingered on the nape of her neck. While he watched, she finished putting the final touches on her face. A dab of eyeshadow, the perfect shade of red lipstick and then hands on his arm, she pushed her feet into three-inch stilettos.

"Do I look good enough to be Mrs. Vittori now?"

A fire licked into his eyes. His arm rose toward her face, slowly, his features tight. But it fell away before it reached her mouth.

She saw the bob of his Adam's apple, the controlled tremor that seemed to shake his powerful body. "Forget all the rubbish the media writes about my affairs, the compare and contrasts, *si*? You're beautiful, and talented, and you could take any one of those women single-handedly."

Any other day, she'd have preened under his praise. But today, it served as a much needed reminder. The research into his love life was a reminder.

He'd never even had a girlfriend for longer than three months.

But for those voting shares, for the sake of the blasted company, he would sign his name next to hers on a piece of paper without even a prenup.

That was like a tiger willingly walking into a cage.

Until she had arrived back in London, until she had heard all the hoopla about his billions, until she had read about his rigid but straightforward tactics when it came to the company, she hadn't appreciated what a big thing that was.

He had billions, an empire he had built piece by piece over the last two decades and he was leaving it open to attack, making it vulnerable by marrying her without the prenup.

Like an eager puppy that returns again and again for affection, Ali couldn't help but think that it was because he trusted her not to come after his fortune.

Maybe just a little bit.

Being the one woman that ruthless Dante Vittori trusted beyond anyone or anything was bound to go to the head of even the most sensible woman between sixteen and sixty, any woman who had a working vagina, any woman who could appreciate having a little glimpse into a powerful and striking man like Dante.

And Ali had never been rational or sensible when it came to Dante.

For a quiet, civil ceremony, there were too many people waiting in the registrar's office. Somehow, Ali had made it without hyperventilating through the ride.

Izzy's gaze sought hers but Ali didn't meet it. There was only so much acting she could do and quiet Izzy would know in a second how this affected her. She and Marco, Dante's head of security, were to be the two witnesses.

Three men stood in the outer office, a lot of paperwork in front of them, and Ali realized they were lawyers. A tall woman and two men stood behind her—the gossip columnist and her team.

"Come," Dante whispered at her ear and Ali followed him inside.

Somehow, she made it through, smiling, shaking the kind registrar's hand. She even laughed vacuously at some thin joke.

And then it was time for the vows.

When the man asked her if she wanted to add anything personal to the preexisting set of vows, Ali wanted to run away. This was wrong. All wrong.

She felt the warmth of Dante's body by her side before he turned her toward him. And slowly, the declaratory words came, more easily than she had thought they would, his gaze holding hers, anchoring her, his broad shoulders her entire world.

"I do solemnly declare that I know not of any lawful impediment why I, Alisha Rajeswari Matta, may not be joined in matrimony to Dante Stefano Vittori."

Steady and clear, she finished her vows.

When Dante spoke, with no inflection or tone, his gaze fixed, each word swept through her with the force of a thunderstorm. Ali trembled all over.

And then he was finishing… "I call upon these persons here present, to witness that I, Dante Stefano Vittori, do take thee, Alisha Rajeswari Matta, to be my lawful wedded wife."

My lawful wedded wife… The words clung to her skin, as if tattooed there.

She took the pen from the waiting registrar and scribbled her name in a flourish.

A second time.

A third time.

By the fifth time, her fingers shook. Sweat beaded on her upper lip. Ali had no idea how she kept it together when, with each scribble of her name, it felt as if she was twining her fate with his.

Okay, yes, she'd never really given much thought to families and weddings in the last few years.

A wedding had always been some future affair, a loving marriage a dream she had put on the back burner while she figured out the hard path she'd chosen for herself. While she figured out how to save her mother's charity. While she made something of herself that would have made her mama and papa, and maybe even Dante proud.

Which was also why it had been so easy to say yes to this blasted arrangement.

But now her breaths rushed in and out, fast and shallow. She focused on them, willing herself to calm down. It didn't help. Her hands trembled. The next few months would be hard enough without lying to herself.

Being Dante's wife—even in name only, even temporarily—meant something to her. Because he was the one man she'd always…what? Admired? Wanted? Lusted over?

What was it that she felt toward him?

Dante went next.

Despite the misgivings in her tummy, she watched mesmerized as he signed his name with a flourish. No shaking fingers for him.

Because this whole thing meant nothing to him.

Except the company, Dante cared about nothing and no one. That had to be her mantra for every waking minute and disturbingly dream-filled nights. She

walked as if in a trance as the registrar wished them
well and they walked out into the lounge. With people,
waiting and watching them.

"Izzy, give me the rings."

Her mouth fell open. "You didn't…"

His big palms landed on her hip, and pulled her up
toward him with the slightest pressure. Heat from his
hands burned through the silk of her dress, stunning
her, stealing her breath. Her hands were trapped between their bodies, on his chest.

His nose was buried in her hair as he whispered,
"Stop looking as if you were trapped in a nightmare."
A thread of impatience and something else colored his
words. He shifted her hair away from her neck. She
knew he was using the thick curtain of her hair to hide
his words but still she trembled all over. His breath was
warm over her bare neck, sending silky ripples down
her spine. "Do a better job unless you want to confirm
I'm sacrificing myself."

He tugged her fingers up and slipped two rings onto
her left ring finger, as casually and as intimately as if
he were buttoning her shirt.

The camera went click, click, click, in tune to her
thundering heart.

The solitaire diamond in its princess setting winked at
her, the accompanying platinum band beautiful in its sim-
plicity. The rings felt like a vow, a bond tying her to him.

Tears filled her eyes and she hurriedly blinked them
back.

God forbid that camera had caught those tears. They

would say she'd cried and gone down on her knees at his feet out of gratitude or some such.

He opened her palm and dropped another ring there. Fingers shaking, Ali somehow managed to hold the ring in two fingers. He extended his hand to her. For the life of her, she couldn't come up with something casual to say, to shrug off the moment.

She looked down at his hand. Blunt, square-tipped nails on elegantly long fingers. Such a small detail. Such an intimate detail.

The Dante database in her brain pinged. God, she was going mental with this. Holding his fingers, she slipped the ring on.

"Now, if we can get a couple of shots of you two kissing," the beige pantsuit said with a smile, "our readers are desperate for more about you two. It would be icing on the cake."

The rest of the reporter's words drifted away into nothingness as Ali's gaze jerked to Dante's.

Shock pulsed through her. Jet-black eyes held hers, curiously devoid of anything. No mockery, no warning. Just waiting for her to follow his lead.

He had known this was coming, had known what the reporter would ask. He'd probably planned it out in his diary the day he'd proposed this arrangement. And yet, he'd left her in the dark.

If he kissed her, if he even touched her, there was no way to hide her desire for him. To hide this madness he stirred up in her. And the thought of rejection in his eyes, or even worse, pity…

But he didn't give her a chance to protest.

Or to think.

Hands on her hips tugged her forward. Dark, fathomless eyes held hers as he bent his head toward her.

Ali could feel herself falling into those eyes, drowning in their intensity. Swimming in the dark depths. Terrified that she'd betray her own longing, she closed her eyes.

Every other sense magnified a thousand times. The world around them—the reporters, the witnesses, the dingy old walls, everything melted away.

Only Dante remained.

"Put your arms around my neck." He sounded needy, husky, hanging on the edge of desperation. She refused, or couldn't curb, her overactive imagination. Her hands crept around his neck.

He smelled like heat and masculine need and dark desires. His hands patted her back, as if to soothe her continuous tremors, up and down until suddenly they were digging into her hips.

His breath hit her mouth in soft strokes, the knot in her belly winding and whirling upon itself.

And then his lips touched hers in a soft, silken glide. Just there and gone, before she could pull a breath. Ali jerked at the contact, nerve endings flaring into life. She tried to jerk away from his hold.

His curse filled her ears. "Shh...*bella mia.*"

One hand settled at the base of her neck, holding her still and he pressed another of those featherlight kisses.

Tease and torment.

An infinitesimal moment after an eternity of longing.

It wasn't enough. A feral groan rippled up through her body as he pressed another kiss. Ali opened her mouth. And the careful swipe of his tongue against his own lips became something else.

Acting on an instinct as old as time and space itself, she slid her tongue against his lush lower lip then dug the tips of her teeth into it.

The tenor of the kiss changed from one breath to the next. Rough hands moved from her hips to her buttocks, cupping, kneading, pressing her close. The sound that tore out of his mouth was growly, hungry, and it lit a spark of hunger in her body.

Ali pressed herself into him and trembled all over again.

He was aroused. He was aroused. Dear God, he was aroused.

His erection was a brand against her belly, his hard thighs cradling hers. His hands crept into her hair, pulled at it until her head was tilted at the perfect angle. Until her mouth was open for his assault.

Dante's mouth. On hers.

Feral. Hungry. Ravenous.

Hot. Hard. Wild.

It wasn't how she'd imagined it would feel. It was a million times better.

He plunged his tongue into her mouth, sliding it against hers, licking, nipping, biting. And then he did it all over again. Again and again.

There was no sense of that self-control, the self-possession that he was known for in his kiss. A torrent of Italian fell from his mouth, gliding over her sensitive skin. Her breasts were heavy, her nipples peaking at the constant rub against his chest.

Her hands clutched his biceps when his tongue swooped in, licking, stroking, nipping and repeating the sensual torture all over again. His hands roamed all over her, kneading, stroking, kindling the spark into an unquenchable fire.

He didn't let her gasp for air. His mouth rubbed up over hers again and again.

Until she was trembling like a leaf against him. Until there was wetness against the soft folds of her sex. Until she splayed her leg around his lean hips and sank into him. That contact was like a jolt of electricity. Liquid fire in her veins.

Until a cough and a whistle and a "Hot damn, they're really into each other" punctured the moment.

Dante wrenched his mouth away from hers, his hands on her shoulders firmly setting her back from him. His breath was harsh, his mouth swollen and dark pink.

Ali had no idea what he barked at Izzy and the rest of them. Had no idea what was up, what was down. Had no idea if she was walking or floating.

She went where he took her.

The hard slam of the door woke her up and she looked out at her surroundings. They were back in his chauffeured limo, cut off from the world. He sat opposite her.

Color burned in those high cheekbones. "It shouldn't have gone that far."

The cutting coldness in his tone pushed Ali out of the sensual fog. She licked her lips and tasted him there. And liked it far too much.

She knew how he felt. She even agreed with him. No good could come out of this attraction. This mutual attraction. This red-hot attraction that wasn't all in her head.

Dante wanted her. Her mind was stuck in that loop.

"If you blame me for it, I'll sink my nails into your pretty face." Good, she sounded steady. Like her knees weren't still quaking. "You orchestrated that whole thing there, so don't you dare blame me if it went off your precious script."

Something dawned in his eyes. For the life of her, Ali didn't know what. Even his remoteness now, as if that kiss hadn't made even a dent in his self-control, couldn't douse the feral satisfaction that ran through her.

The dynamic between them shifted and swirled in the luxurious interior of his car.

"One kiss doesn't mean anything, Alisha."

She fell back down to earth with a vicious thud even as she told herself the same thing. "No, it doesn't."

But it meant everything.

The taste of him lingered on her lips, the press of his fingers on her hips a burn.

It meant Dante saw her as a woman.

It meant Dante wanted her desperately.

It meant Dante and his self-control could go on a hike when she was near.

It meant for the first time in her life, the power in their relationship was fluid.

She wasn't foolish enough to pursue this thing, but man, it felt good to have it. She let a sassy smile curve her mouth, determined to come out on top. No matter that she would relive that kiss a million times from here to the end of eternity.

No matter when she went to bed tonight, her wedding night as it turned out, she was going to play that in her head while she got herself off. In the twisted world that they were inhabiting right now, she actually had the right to him, didn't she?

Lawful wedded husband and wife and all that...

"What are you thinking?" he asked, that something flashing in his eyes again. And this time, Ali recognized it for what it was.

Dante's desire for her, despite his self-control.

"That after my X-rated dreams about you for so long, this time, I have real material to work with tonight. Conveniently, my wedding night," she said, brazening it out.

The curse that fell from his mouth was filthy and long and ricocheted around the leather interior. It was music to her ears.

Ali laughed, the power that rocked through her washing away the sense of inadequacy that had haunted her for so long.

Color bled into his high cheekbones, his eyes filled with dark desire as he held hers. He was imagining what she'd said, he knew that, she knew that.

Ali refused to look away.

"Alisha, if you—"

"What's in my mind is not in your control, Dante. Let it go."

Another short, pithy curse this time. "You really thrive on it, don't you? You have to control everything around you."

He nodded and looked away. "*Si*. It's... I can't undo it now. This is a marriage on paper, Alisha."

Warning reverberated in his words and hit her right in the solar plexus. But nothing could take away the high she was riding. "You said to control the narrative, *si*? So, I've got it. You fell in love with me on one of your visits while trying to pin me down all these years. Desperately. I led you on a merry chase all around the world and finally, I let you catch me.

"That kiss says that perfectly. I want to be the star of this story. I want to be the woman who brought Dante Vittori to his knees in love. And when this is over, I will be the one who walked away. Capisce?"

She stared at him defiantly, daring him to contradict her. Seconds felt like eons. Whatever vulnerability she had felt earlier, whatever emotion had gripped her, lifted as she wrested control of the situation.

She would be the one to walk away, she'd make sure of that. And in the meantime, she was going to have a hell of a lot of fun poking the sexy, gruff bear.

His gaze searched her, as if he was seeing her for the first time. As if she'd morphed into something he didn't understand right in front of his eyes.

And it was a power trip for her.

CHAPTER SEVEN

THE TASTE OF Alisha's mouth—so potently sweet, so addictively warm—clung to Dante's lips even a fortnight later. Through meetings with the Japanese team over negotiating a multibillion-dollar contract supplying steel spread over ten years, through board meetings that he and Ali attended together to present a united front to Nitin and the rest of the board members, through endless evenings when Dante caught her in the sitting room of his flat before she disappeared into the darkroom on the lower floor.

She'd been so dainty, so fragile, trembling like a leaf when he'd clasped his arm around her waist, when he'd pressed his palm into her slender back to pull her closer…but her passion had been voracious, honest, a force of its own.

He'd just meant to touch his lips to hers in a quick press. He'd meant to keep it platonic.

But thinking Alisha would behave when she could wreak mischief on the whole situation, when she could use the moment to challenge him, to pay him back for surprising her with the press, had been his first mistake.

Imagining that the attraction between them would wither away if he continued to ignore it, his second.

Just as Dante had predicted, the media and the world exploded at the shots he'd had his PR team release.

The Kiss, as it was being referred to by the entire world, had taken the media by storm.

Except the kiss hadn't turned out to be the perfectly set up shot he'd planned. No, it was a minute-long clip that had gone viral already on a million websites, as one of the most candidly romantic shots.

Especially because he looked ravenously hungry for her, because in his adult life, he'd never once lost himself in a woman like that. Ali had gotten what she wanted. The whole world believed she'd brought him to his knees.

Dante couldn't even blame the press for sensationalizing the story. The defiant tilt of Ali's chin as she pressed herself to his body brazenly, the hunger and passion in that moment... His lower body tightened every time he watched it—like a teenager watching his first porn video.

One glance at the clip and he had an erection.

Dios mio, it consumed him night and day. It came to him when he saw her lithe body in those skimpy clothes she paraded around in in the flat. It came to him when they were forced into physical intimacy at any public outing they had to attend as a couple.

It came to him when he simply looked at her mouth.

His entire adult life, he'd thrived on control in every aspect of his life and that meant his libido too. The women he'd chosen to take to his bed—he'd never let lust drive those choices. His affairs—even the short-term ones—hadn't involved wanting one woman so badly.

They had been more of a quest for release.

Wanting Alisha of course fell into none of the principles he lived by. If it had been just a physical attraction to her—if it was a matter of an itch needing to be scratched because of their history, because, in his entire life, Alisha was the one woman who never seemed to be cowed by him, who challenged his control, who with delicious defiance came toe-to-toe with him—it would have been different.

If she had continued to tease and torment him, if she had used the knowledge of his desire for her as some kind of weapon—damn it, it almost seemed like he half expected and half wanted her to do it—then it would have been another matter altogether.

No, the equally ferocious depth of her desire for him had been a one-off.

In a strange role reversal, she seemed to be the one conducting herself perfectly, a charming socialite wife, a smart charity hostess in the public eye and a polite, courteous stranger under his roof.

The charity was growing from strength to strength now that she had thrown herself into it. She had used the news of their engagement to raise its profile, make connections. Her photography she still held pretty close to her chest. He was getting more and more curious about it, he'd even told her he wouldn't comment on or mock something that was simply a hobby, but she refused to let him see even a single portrait.

An empty attraction to a woman he didn't quite admire or even like was an easy matter. But the more days that passed by, the more he saw a different side to Alisha.

The way she'd thrown herself into it over the past couple of weeks was eye-opening.

He'd even dropped in one afternoon, with a valid reason in hand—more papers to sign confirming that she was releasing the voting shares to him—at the office space she'd rented. Alisha had been deep in conversation with the new accounts manager she'd hired, looking at a presentation he knew she'd slaved over for the last week about expansion plans she wanted to take up in the next two years with the new infusion of cash—a dream that her mother, Shanti, had put on hold after she'd left Neel.

He'd found himself smiling when he dropped by in the middle of the day sometimes and found her at the piano, playing old Hindi melodies that he'd heard Neel play many years ago. And when she wasn't working on the charity, she escaped into her darkroom. He'd been tempted, more than once, to ask her if she was hiding from him. From them.

But asking her meant acknowledging what they were both trying to deny. It meant asking himself a question he didn't want to probe within himself.

Restlessness plaguing him, he walked to the portrait that hung on the wall in his office. He and Neel had been interviewed for a *Business Week* article and had posed for the picture.

He looked at the man who'd given him the chance to make something of himself. The man who'd taken him at his word, the man who'd seen and nurtured his work ethic and not the dark shadow of his father's crime. Neel had given him a chance at a second life, a better life, a new path.

Alisha was Neel's daughter.

And so Alisha would always be forbidden to Dante, especially for the sort of relationships he had with women.

He had easily bartered for her voting shares because those shares would be used to drive the best interests of the company, but kissing her, touching her, thinking these thoughts of her…

There was a spike in his heartbeat when his phone rang and Alisha's face lit up the screen. He let it go to voice mail.

Two minutes later, a series of pings came through. An almost juvenile thrill went through him at the thought of those waiting texts.

Spending tonight @ MM

He frowned. MM meant Matta Mansion. The house where she'd refused to stay just a few weeks ago.

The next text was a series of emojis with cake and wine bottles and champagne glasses.

FYI Getting drunk. Won't return tonight. Don't freak out. Send Marco tmrw morn. Good night, Dante.

And then a kiss emoji.

He smiled, her irreverence coming through in her texts.

But he didn't know whether it was simply an FYI as she claimed, or a red herring to hide what she was really up to. He hadn't missed the fact that she'd been unusually subdued yesterday night too.

He noticed the missed calls from his mother. She called him only a few times a year.

Hurriedly, he looked at the date. He left the office, even as reams of paperwork awaited him, without second thought.

He couldn't leave her alone, tonight of all nights.

With its white marble facade and once beautifully maintained grounds, Matta Mansion greeted Dante like an old friend. *Dios mio*, he shouldn't have let the house fall into such a state of neglect.

Even though Shanti had already been gone for years with Ali in tow, he knew Neel had kept it in great condition with the hope that she'd come back to him.

Dante had moved out after Vikram had died in that crash and Ali had left London. Neel had treated him as another son, but it hadn't felt right to be there without them.

A lot of good things had happened in his life here. He'd found solid ground to stand upon, belief in himself after his life crashed and burned, all thanks to Neel's generosity.

But Alisha… For the first time since she had walked into the mansion—a thirteen-year-old girl with a haunting ache in her eyes and a defiant distrust of her father, her brother and himself—he saw it from her point of view.

How scared and lost she must have been. How, lost in his own grief, every action Neel had taken regarding her had been neglectful and alienating and sometimes downright cruel.

Neel had never hugged his daughter. He'd never reassured her that he wanted her in his life. And when she'd started acting out, he'd cut communications, he'd had Dante implement his decisions for Alisha.

Dante had been blind to it all.

His wife, Shanti's, death had hit his mentor hard. Dante had never pried into why she'd walked out on Neel with her daughter in tow. He had automatically assumed that it had been somehow Shanti's fault.

God, even then, he'd been a distrusting cynic.

You three had each other. Who did I have?

They were there for me when I was lost and alone.

Those words haunted Dante as he slid his Mercedes through the electronic gates and into the courtyard.

She had no good memories of this place. And yet, she was here tonight.

For once, Dante wanted to be what Alisha needed. He wanted to care for her.

What he felt in his chest didn't feel like some misguided sense of loyalty. The knot of anticipation as he walked in through the foyer and took the stairs up the winding staircase didn't feel like responsibility.

The thrill that coursed through his blood, the swift punch of desire tightening every muscle as he opened the door to her old bedroom and found Alisha on the floor, leaning against her white princess bed, her head bowed, her knees pulled up to her chest, didn't feel like pity for a girl he should have tried to understand better back then.

She'd turned on the lamp on the side table next to her and the soft pink walls created a glow around her leaving the rest dark. A bottle of Scotch and a couple of glasses lay in front of her. In her hand was a framed photograph of her mother, more on the floor.

Of Neel with Dante and Vikram.

Of Neel with her, both of them stiff and unbending.

Of Dante and her, at one of the parties that Neel had insisted on throwing.

She looked so painfully alone that a wave of tenderness swept through him. But even that couldn't arrest the swift rush of desire.

A pale pink spaghetti strap top and shorts, her usual attire, bared her shoulders. In the glow of the lamp, contrasted by the surrounding darkness, her skin, silky and smooth, beckoned his touch. Her hair rippled every time she took a long breath.

Unwilling to disturb her, he looked around the room he hadn't entered in years.

A room of her own, built with a domed ceiling and fairy lights, handcrafted furniture custom ordered for her, couture clothes and jewelry, antiques, priceless Indian pieces acquired at royal auctions, modern, light pieces that Shanti herself had favored—Neel had given Ali everything a princess would expect.

But not what she'd so desperately needed.

Affection. Understanding. Love.

Suddenly, in this room she'd perceived as a cage, Dante saw Ali for who she truly was.

The glimpses of vulnerability beneath the brazen fa-cade, the reason she was slaving to save her mother's charity, the very reason she'd accepted his proposal… Ali lived and breathed emotion as much as he scorned and avoided it.

But even that didn't send him running.

She looked up at him, and her eyes grew wide. The long line of her throat was bare, the pulse jumping rap-idly. "What are you doing here?"

"I wanted to see—"

"If I was dragging your good name through mud and dirt, emboldened by my father's Scotch? Throw-ing a wild party with a lot of naked people gyrating on the floor?"

Once those taunting words would have riled him no end. Now, all he saw was the vulnerability she hid under the affected defiance. He removed his jacket, draped it on the bed and joined her on the floor.

She stared at his feet and then up, her gaze touching every inch of his body. *Cristo*, had she any idea what she was doing to him?

"You remembered to take off your shoes and socks?"

Something mundane. To fill the silence. "Of course. This was my home for years."

"I…want to be alone. Now that you have confirmed that I won't cause any bad PR, you can leave."

He undid his cuffs and rested his hands on his knees. Her eyes followed his every move, her disbelief and something else coloring the silence. "I thought I should join the celebration. How many did we celebrate to-gether?"

"Seven, eight?" Her fingers were tightly furled in her lap. She crisscrossed her legs, giving him a view of her toned thighs. Feeling like a Peeping Tom, he looked away. "I hated each and every one of them, just so you know. That first year, I thought at least for my birthday, he would be mine, just mine. Instead he forced me to share it with you."

"Neel held me up as an ideal, demanded that you treat me like the demigod I am and so you hated me on principle."

She made a sound that was half snort and half laugh.

He liked that sound. He liked when she was her flippant, brazen self.

The moment made the thick mass of her hair hit his neck and his shoulders. The side of her grazed him and he tightened every muscle in his body to minimize the contact. He tensed against the pleasure barreling through him.

Still, he didn't leave.

"It wasn't all just on principle, Dante. You…you made it—"

He took her hand and squeezed, guilt sitting on his chest like an anvil. He'd been the recipient of a self-indulgent parent's neglect and yet he hadn't seen the same in her plight. "I'm sorry for not seeing how alienated and alone you felt in your own home, thanks to me."

The stillness that came over her was like a seismic shift. Except she didn't explode. He saw the sheen of tears in her eyes and turned away. She wouldn't want him to see her like that.

A strange, unbidden, unwanted sentimentality swirled through him tonight and he didn't want to feed it any more fuel. Seeing Ali in pain, he was sure, would qualify as fuel.

"I… It wasn't all you," she whispered. "You just made an easy target. I despised you because you were so close to him and I took every chance I could to show you. And him."

"Your father was a man with a great vision. But he wasn't perfect. I've been blind to that."

Another stretch of silence.

"I'm sorry I was so horrible to you. That I burned your Armani suit with those Diwali sparklers, and for shredding important contracts."

"What about the terror you unleashed on my girl-friend? Melissa? Melody?"

"Meredith," she corrected with a smirk. "She deserved it. She was horribly snooty." When he looked at her, she turned her face away. "I had the most humon-gous crush on you, which is really twisted given how much I hated you."

"I'm not sure if I guessed that or not. You were… hard to understand."

Her shoulders shook as she laughed and buried her face in her hands.

"Pour me a glass, *si*?"

Her fingers trembled as she lifted the decanter and poured him a drink. He took the tumbler from her hands before it slipped to the carpet and turned so that he could better see her.

Her skin glowed golden, the thin bridge of her nose

flaring. Her mouth…just the sight of her lips sent desire crashing through him. *When had want become need?*

He raised his glass. "Happy birthday, Ali. What are you, eighteen now?"

"I'm twenty-six," she said, bumping him with her shoulder. "You, on the other hand, are what, a hundred and twenty?" When he didn't answer, she clinked her glass against his. "Happy birthday, Dante."

He took a sip of the Scotch.

They stayed like that for he didn't know how long. That current of awareness still pervaded the air, but there was also something else. A comfortable silence. All that shared history finally untangled enough to realize that there was a bond between them.

A new beginning, maybe. A fragile connection.

Something he hadn't known weighed on his chest for so long seemed to lift. She was her papa's legacy even if she desperately denied it. And she'd always been his responsibility, even before he'd made her take his name.

The Scotch was both fiery and smooth as it went down her throat and settled into a warm fire in Ali's veins. It seemed to open up her senses even more, as if the awareness of Dante sitting next to her, his thighs grazing hers slightly, the masculine scent of him—sweat and cologne and him an irresistible combination—wasn't enough.

The last thing she'd expected when she'd texted him was to see him here. All day she'd been in a melancholy mood that she hadn't been able to shake. The charity gala her team was putting together to raise more funds or even the meeting with an agent she desperately wanted to sign—nothing could hold her interest. In the end, she'd called in sick to both, and drifted from place to place all over London, ending up at a quaint coffee shop she used to visit when she'd shared a flat nearby with two girls.

She liked to think of it as her grounding year.

She'd moved away from Matta Mansion, walked away from her father and Vicky and Dante. It had been the hardest thing she'd ever done but also the most liberating.

But even the coffee shop that was like a warm, old friend hadn't been able to chase away the blues.

She was lonely.

She'd been lonely for a long time now, ever since her mother's death. The last few years had been better. She'd surrounded herself with friends who cared about her. She'd filled her days with meaningful charity work wherever she lived, in those lulls between her photography stints, but being back in London was unsettling.

No, it wasn't London.

It wasn't even this house that her father had built for her mother when they'd been newly married, where painful memories dwelled.

No, this ache in her chest, this constant thrum under her skin, was because of the man next to her. But she couldn't take a step toward him, she couldn't bear it if he rejected her, even if this time she wanted to be with him for all the right reasons. She wanted to be with him as a woman who understood herself and her desires and her own shortcomings.

She liked him. A lot.

She liked her father's protégé who was ten years older than she was and knew all her flaws and vulnerabilities.

She liked the man she'd had a crush on for years.

She liked the man she was married to. If it weren't so tragic, it would be comic.

Her thoughts swirled, her senses stirred. It was exhausting to feel like this all the time. She couldn't—

"Are you going to tell me what brought you here tonight?"

She whirled the glass in her hand, watching light reflect and refract through the golden liquid. "Do you really want to know?"

"Yes, Alisha. When I ask you a question, usually it's because I want to know the answer."

"I don't… I was feeling melancholy. So I took the bus around most of London today, just…reminiscing. I ended up at this coffee shop I used to go to with friends after I left…to live on my own. I ran into my ex there."

He didn't move or even bat an eyelid. But she sensed the stillness that came over him as surely as if a cold frost had blown into the room. "Jai?"

He didn't remember his own girlfriend's name but he remembered Jai? "Yes."

"Ah…you're pining over him." Was there an edge to those words that she could detect beneath the control?

"It was a shock to see him, yes. But out of all the decisions I made then, Jai was… He was a good influence on me. He made me see that just because I didn't do that apprenticeship didn't mean I had to give up photography. When he saw me today, he gave me a quick hug, all open smiles. Talked about his start-up, congratulated me on my news—"

"Your news? Did that agent sign you on? Why didn't you tell me?"

Putting her glass away, Ali stood up, scooted onto the bed and leaned against the headboard. Dante stood up in a lithe move, a tic in his tight jaw as he looked at her.

"What? I'm getting a crick in my neck turning to see your face and my bottom is falling asleep on the floor." She patted the place next to her on the bed and smiled, faking a brazenness she didn't feel. "I won't bite, Dante."

He said nothing. Just stared at her for a few more seconds, then sat down near her feet.

"I haven't heard from the agent. I actually haven't sent him my portfolio yet."

"Why not? You've been in your darkroom for hours and hours this week." He took her hand in his. "You are scared of being rejected."

She shrugged. Yes, she was. "No one's ever seen my work."

"And you'll never know where you stand unless you send it." He looked at her hand in his, his voice husky, his head bent down. Her fingers itched to sink into his hair. "What was Jai congratulating you about then?"

"Our wedding. He was congratulating me on…" She compulsively turned the ring on her finger. "This." Jai had been genuinely happy for her, that she'd finally achieved her heart's desire, he'd said.

When she'd looked at him blankly, he had smiled understandingly.

You think I didn't know? I liked you, Ali, really. But even for the few months we were together you had too much baggage. Too much... You were fixated on him. On Dante. He was all you talked about. His personal life, his relationship with your father, his relationship with you. It was clear that Dante would always be the primary man in your life. You were half in love with him, as much as you continuously claimed that you hated him.

She'd always wondered why Jai had ended their relationship. But she'd moved on easily. She'd wanted to travel, she'd wanted to focus on photography. Today, his answer had shaken her.

She'd been fixated on Dante back then, yes, but that wasn't love. What the hell did she know about love anyway?

For the rest of the day, Jai's words had haunted her. Now she saw it.

The melancholy that had gripped her, it was an ache to be with Dante.

To spend time with him in comfortable silence like now, or trading snappy comebacks, to discuss stoicism and pop culture—three guesses who was into which—to laugh with him, to understand what drove that razor-sharp mind and fueled that ambition, to touch him, to have the freedom to run her hand over his cheek whenever she wanted, to sink her fingers into his thick hair, to press her mouth to his in a quick kiss every time he got that brooding look in his eyes...

To be just a woman with him. A woman he liked and respected and wanted. Their lives were intricately twined now, for the first time seeing each other clearly and her feelings consumed her.

She pressed the heels of her palms to her eyes. "You were right. I…I think I'll move back here. There's just more room here and once the novelty of our announcement dies down, it's not like the media can see if we're spending our nights together in one room. I mean, in the same house. We both work insane hours anyway."

In the dim light of the lamp, his scowl was downright ferocious. "What?"

"As big as your flat is, it's…like living in each other's pockets. This way, we'll have more freedom, more… space."

"More space to do what, precisely? See your ex again? Should we expect him to come knocking on the door any moment now? Is that why you wanted me to leave?"

She jumped off the bed, fury burning away that achy longing. "That's unfair. The last thing I'd do is have a secret affair while the whole world is crowing about our wedding as the most romantic thing in the decade. Not that you deserve my…fidelity. I just can't do this anymore."

She turned to leave the room, to leave his unfair comments to himself, but he grabbed her arm.

Ali ended up against him, his legs straddling her hips, her hands on his chest. He rubbed her back gently, his breath feathering over her forehead. The scent of him made her skin tight. The incredible warmth of his body made hers hum.

She wanted to stay like that the entire night. An entire lifetime.

His hands were gentle as he clasped her cheek, a slumbering warmth in his eyes. "If it's the agent, I'll make some calls. If it's the charity that worries you, don't. And if it's the media scrutiny that's bothering you, it will die down soon.

"You're…you're so much his daughter, Alisha. Driven and grounded. I was wrong to think you were a spoiled princess. Whatever the problem is, I'll fix it. I owe it to Neel to do right by you."

Just like that, he tramped all over Ali's budding feelings. She didn't want his loyalty or his sympathy because she was her father's daughter. She wanted him to see her. Alisha. "It's you." The words tumbled out of her mouth. "You make this all strange and wrong and hard. I feel like I signed away more than those blasted voting shares."

Shock filled his eyes. Slowly he pulled his hand away. "I would never harm you, Ali."

She nodded. He didn't get it. He would never get it. Ambition and goals and reputations, those things he understood. Matters of the heart were a different matter.

She was terrified that slowly, irrevocably Dante was stealing hers. And if she didn't stop it, if she didn't steel herself against him, if she was foolish enough to offer it to him, he would crush it into a thousand pieces.

Still, she asked. "Are you happy to pretend that kiss didn't change anything between us?"

After a long time, he blinked slowly, tension pulling at his mouth. "Yes."

She fisted her hands. "I don't have your self-control, nor do I want to suppress every little thing I feel when I genuinely like you. I can't live with you and pretend as if I don't want to do this."

"Do what?"

"This."

She pressed her mouth to his, every breath in her bracing for him to push her away. His lips were soft and firm. Scooting closer on her knees, hands on his shoulders, she tasted the skin just under his ear, felt the shudder that moved through his hard body.

He tasted like heat, like heaven, like homecoming.

When he gripped her hands to push her away, she trailed her tongue up to his jaw, alternating with nips and bites until she reached the sexy hollow of his throat. She pressed her tongue against that hollow, feeling his pulse inside her. Feeling the power of his body inside her. "Tell me the truth just once. Tell me you don't want me and I'll do whatever you ask. I'll never talk about this again."

Without waiting for an answer, she nipped his skin, hard, long, with her teeth. He growled, a drawn-out erotic sound. The tips of her breasts grazed his chest and she let his hard body take even more of her weight. Tipsy, drunk, delirious, she felt a buzz at his harsh breaths. She pushed her hand down his broad chest, over the hard ridge of his abdomen to his belt and below. His breath was like the bellows of a forge in her ears.

Her hand found the waistband of his trousers and then the zipper. Belly clenching, she traced the hard ridge pressing up beneath the fabric. Up and down, just with one finger, until he grew harder and longer beneath her touch. Nerves tight, she covered him with her palm. His shaft twitched against her hand, making her mouth dry.

God, an incredibly unbearable erotic rush filled her very veins. He was that hard for her. She could have died and gone to heaven, just for that.

He gripped her wrist like a tight manacle, stilling her. But he didn't push her away. And Ali pushed her advantage.

Sinking her fingers into his hair, straddling his hard thighs, she pressed shamelessly closer. Their mingled groans rent the air as his hardness pressed against her sex at just the right spot.

Rough hands tugged her by her hair and then he was kissing her with a ferocious hunger that matched her own. Teeth banged as he plunged his tongue inside her mouth and dueled with hers. His tongue thrust and withdrew from her mouth, making her sex clench. Whorls of sensation built in her lower belly. The kiss whipped her senses into a frenzy.

Mouth open, he left damp patches on her throat. His lips soothed while his teeth bit, and soon Ali was sobbing for more. She pulled his hands from her hips to her breasts, the tips aching for his touch. "Please, Dante... more."

She didn't care that she was begging. That she was raw and vulnerable and all the things she'd promised herself she wouldn't be with him. But whatever madness had her in its grip seemed to hold him too.

Still holding her gaze, he brought his mouth down to her neck, to the upper curve of her breasts. "Pull your T-shirt up."

Fingers trembling, Ali did it. He traced the seam of the white lace with his tongue, a dark fire in his eyes. Transfixed, Ali watched as his rough mouth found the peak jutting up lewdly against the thin silk fabric.

His fingers were so unbearably gentle when he pulled the lace cup down. Her breast popped out, jutted up by the tight wire of her bra, the peak tight and begging for his attention.

Breath hung in her throat as he closed those sinuous lips around it. She jerked her hips against his when he pressed his tongue against her nipple and grazed his teeth over its surface.

She moaned, and twisted her hips in mindless abandon when he sucked her nipple and the curve of her breast into his mouth. The pulls of his mouth, the thrust of his hips, the press of him against her core…sensation upon sensation built in her lower belly. She was moaning, she was panting. He used his teeth against the plump tip and Ali felt like she was lifting out of her body.

She thrust against him, shameless in her pursuit for release, her thighs in a death grip around his hips, her fingers holding his mouth to her chest, her heart beating like a fluttering bird against its cage.

Relentless waves of pleasure beat down over her, drenching her sex in wetness. Her throat felt hoarse from all the screaming. She hid her face in his shoulder, a strange joy fluttering through her veins.

A torrent of curses ripped from Dante, puncturing

the deafening silence around them with a contained violence. He dislodged her onto the bed.

He ran a hand through his hair, standing against the door, his chest heaving, a sheen of perspiration on his forehead. His hair was sticking out at all angles because she'd pulled and tugged at it to her heart's content while he'd made her body sing.

"*Cristo*, this is your childhood bedroom, in his house!"

The aftershocks of her orgasm unfurled through her pelvis even as tears filled her eyes.

No, damn it, she wasn't going to cry. She'd wanted what had happened, she wanted a lot more. But neither was she going to enter into a cycle of self-pity. She wasn't going to beg him to give this thing between them a chance.

She'd shown him, told him what she wanted. Now, it was up to him. She had far too much self-respect to beg a man to act on what he clearly felt for her.

Ali pulled herself up on the bed.

His head jerked up at that moment, the shadow of his hunger for her still in his eyes.

Dark color slashed his razor-sharp cheekbones as that hot gaze drifted down to her breasts. Her nipples were swollen and tight from his fingers, from his mouth. His evening shadow had left a mark on the upper slopes.

Chin tilted, Ali faced him. Her insides were a gooey, painful knot, while her hands shook. Holding his gaze, she hooked her bra together and pulled the straps into place, adjusting the cups at the front. It was a push-up bra, designed to create cleavage.

And still, he stared. She looked around for her T-shirt and pulled it on. Then she raked her hands through her hair, hair he'd tangled by pulling it while he plundered her mouth.

There wasn't a part of her body on which he hadn't left an impression. Just the memory of his erection rocking into her was enough to send a sweet ache between her legs.

"Ali—"

"It happened. I'm not sorry it did. With all the pheromones running wild in my system right now, I think it's impossible to regret that." She held his gaze, for the first time since she'd seen him as a thirteen-year-old, hiding nothing from him. "It was the most amazing experience of my life with a man I like, I respect and I want. Don't cheapen it, don't tell me why it's wrong. Don't take this away from me."

He walked toward her with each of her words. Ali flinched when he clasped her cheek reverently, when he rubbed his thumb over her lower lip. "Do you know, that's the first time in a long while that I've forgotten what I stand for? Seeing you come apart like that…" Naked desire filled his eyes. "I've never lost my mind like that. I've never wanted a woman so much that it's messing with my work, never. The passion in your kiss, the honest desire in your eyes, the sounds you make when you climax…they will haunt me for the rest of my life. For all my fortune, you're the one thing I can't afford."

Ali braced herself, like a leaf in a cool autumn wind. Whatever emotion she'd spied in his eyes drained away, leaving that cool, unflappable mask. "You and me, this can't go anywhere. I don't do relationships and doing this with you, when I know I can't give you anything else…that will just make me the kind of man I spent my whole life trying not to be."

"What kind of a man would that be? A man who feels emotion, a man who clearly cares for those around him, a man capable of far more than he lets himself give?" Ali demanded. Her own strength surprised her. But then, Dante had always been capable of pushing her.

His eyes flared, something almost like fear in them. God, she was being delusional. What could a man like Dante fear?

"I deserve at least an explanation after that orgasm you gave me."

This time it wasn't fear, but self-disgust. "If I take you tonight, just because I want you, because you want me, knowing that all I can give you is a cheap, torrid affair under the guise of this marriage, it's a betrayal of all the trust your dad gave me."

"Papa has nothing to do with this."

"Neel will always have everything to do with me and you, Ali," he shouted the words at her. Self-disgust painted his features harsh. "If I screw you against the wall, here in his house, it makes me the same selfish bastard as my father was."

"Jesus, Dante, your father fleeced thousands of euros from innocents. How can you say you're the same?"

"I'll be the same because you're innocent and I'll have given in to my basest desires. And all I'll do is take what you give and then discard you when I tire of you. What I want from you—the only thing I want from you—are those voting shares. And you've already given them to me."

The cruel finality of his words pierced Ali like nothing else she'd ever experienced. How could it hurt so much when it was what she'd expected?

When she didn't really know what she wanted from him?

It felt like giving up but she nodded anyway. Survival instinct took over.

She stiffened when he took her hands in his and pulled her into his arms. The tenderness of his embrace stole her breath. Earlier, it had been the way he'd played her body, made her mindless, and now this side of him...

Who knew there was so much depth to the hard man he showed the world? Who knew that even his rejection would only make her like him even more?

She felt his mouth at her temple, the long breath he drew in her hair, the slight vibrations that seemed to shake his shoulders. Her arms went around his waist loosely, for he was the safest place she'd found in a long time. "I understand why you want to leave the flat. But for now, for tonight, will you please come home with me, Alisha? I can't... It would eat me up to leave you here. Do this for me. *Por favor, bella mia.*"

Ali laughed into his neck, even as her tears seeped out and soaked into his skin. Raw vulnerability cloaked her and still, it seemed what had happened, what he said couldn't happen, couldn't puncture the bond that had formed between them.

"What?"

Tilting her head back, she looked at him. Stared into his eyes. Her chest ached at the concern she saw in them. How had she ever thought him uncaring? "I didn't think you knew that word."

He smiled back at her, lines at his eyes, teeth flashing. "I know it." His gaze swept over her face, as if he couldn't help himself. "I just didn't think there would come a day when I would say it to you."

Still smiling, Alisha withdrew from his hold. Shying her gaze away, she packed up her things into her tote bag. "Just for that, I'll make sure you say it again and again to me. In fact, I'll make sure, somehow, I make you beg, Dante."

She walked out of her teenage bedroom without looking back, feeling as if she'd grown a thousand years in just one evening, wishing Vikram was here to hug her, wishing Papa was here to hold her in her confusion, wishing she weren't falling for Dante.

Wishing, once again, in the very same house like she'd done all those years ago, that she could change Dante's mind, that she was enough, wishing he cared about her more than he did.

CHAPTER EIGHT

IT SEEMED TO Dante that the universe or some karmic superpower was conspiring against him.

What he'd done with Ali, to Ali, in her bedroom, of all places... The memory of her flushed face, the image of her lush breasts in his hand, the sensation of those brown tips so hard on his tongue, the wildness of her body as she rocked into him and found her pleasure... *Dios mio*, it haunted him in the fortnight he'd spent in Tokyo on business.

Even in his dreams, Ali was there, taunting him, teasing him, the trusting smile on her lips, the raw desire in those eyes just as arousing as the invitation of her naked limbs.

Until he'd driven her to his flat that night, and bid her good-night at her bedroom door, he'd been terrified that she would refuse him. That he had crossed a line he never should have, that she wouldn't forgive him for his seesawing behavior.

No trip had ever felt so long. Because he'd never had anything to come home to before.

When he'd returned late at midnight, she'd already

been in her bedroom. Somehow, he'd buried the urge to knock, to check that she was really in there. Even though his security team had assured him that she was.

This morning, he had another important meeting with the shareholders. He canceled it.

There was a ruckus involving the Japanese firm and some miscommunication about production schedule and delivery dates between his team and their team. A ten-billion-dollar contract and thousands of new jobs hinged on the deal he had negotiated.

Instead of the usual urgency to smooth out the knots, all he felt was a strange tiredness for his job. *Cristo*, he'd been working nonstop for almost twenty years and this morning he wanted to damn it all to hell.

It had taken Izzy a few tries—at the end of which she'd remarked on his distracted mood—to tell him that all of his management team was sitting on tenterhooks, waiting for his wrath for such a major communications blunder. They were right, he didn't tolerate sloppiness or inefficiency in himself, or his teams. They went through rigorous training and usually his employee base, especially the upper management team, were people who'd been with him for years. And if a mistake of this proportion had been made, the person responsible would have informed him of it immediately and taken corrective steps.

In the end, Dante had figured it out.

It was all Nitin's doing. His petty little revenge was causing havoc. He had been attending meetings he hadn't been invited to behind Dante's back, promising to take the lead on communications and then dropping the ball, leaving some unsuspecting newcomer to take the fire all the while their Japanese client waited for an important communication. It was exactly the kind of games that had made Neel distrust his brother wholly, that had made him try to keep Nitin's corporate decision-making ability severely limited.

That Dante had unequivocally taken a controlling stake in Matta Steel after acquiring Ali's voting shares was a bitter pill for Nitin to swallow.

It had taken Dante longer than it would normally have taken him to figure it out, and to come up with a strategy for how to react appropriately. That morning he'd skipped his usual run, poured himself coffee—coffee he'd automatically made to Ali's liking—and sat at the breakfast bar waiting for her to show up.

Izzy's shock had been palpable on the video call when he'd informed her he intended to work from home that day. Especially with the situation being what it was at work.

But for the first time in his life, he couldn't focus on work. He couldn't think of anything other than facing Ali this morning. Of how to make her stay. He didn't want her at the big, empty mansion with all the sad memories dragging her down. He wouldn't have a moment's rest thinking of her there alone. The loneliness in her eyes—it was the same thing he'd spied in his own eyes before he'd come to live with Neel. But where he had channeled all the powerlessness and the rage he'd felt back then into ambition, into freezing his emotions, Ali was the opposite.

She lived bravely. Everywhere she went, she spread her love and generosity around.

The protectiveness he felt toward her was so new and so intense that he felt a restless urgency in his veins. The idea of her leaving this flat, of leaving London while he'd been gone had consumed him.

The sound of her bedroom door opening jerked his head up. Instead of the shorts and sleeveless T-shirts he'd come to expect from her, she was dressed formally in a fitted dress shirt that hugged her high breasts, a lovely contrast against her brown skin, and black trousers that showcased her long legs. Pink stilettos added a pop of color—that signature Alisha layer to her serious outfit. Her hair fell like a silky curtain to the middle of her back, light gold tints in it catching the weak sun filtering through the high bay window.

Those strands had felt like pure raw silk in his hands that night and he had to fist his hands to fight that urge now.

He watched silently as she placed her jacket and a portfolio bag on the sofa in the living room. There wasn't even a token protest in his mind that he was obsessed with her. Then she checked her cell phone and slid it back into her bag.

She pulled out her left hand and stared at her fingers. She fiddled with the two rings, the princess-cut diamond glittering at him even across the distance. Every muscle in his body knotted as he forced himself to stay quiet.

She pressed a hand to her nape, giving him the lovely lines of her profile. With a soft sigh, she took both the rings off her finger, stared at them a little longer and then slipped them into her handbag.

A roar of denial built through him. He wanted to demand she put those rings back on, he wanted to sink his fingers into her hair and hold her for his kiss, he wanted to throw her over his shoulder and claim his right over her mind, body and soul...

The force of those urges left him stunned.

In just a matter of seconds, he saw his whole life—the life he'd methodically created for himself, the future he'd always envisioned—fall apart like a stack of cards.

He wanted Alisha with a depth of desire he couldn't understand.

He wanted his rings on her finger.

He was already obsessed with the way she leveled those beautiful eyes at him—sometimes in fury, sometimes with laughter, sometimes with such naked, honest desire that it felled him at the knees.

He didn't want her running away again from the charity, from London.

He didn't want her alone in some corner of the world.

He didn't want her running away from him.

And the only way he could have her, was if she was truly his wife.

Ali walked into the kitchen and stilled at the sight of Dante sitting at the gleaming quartz breakfast bar. Usually he left for work at the alarmingly inhumane hour of six thirty having finished his run, his breakfast and his shower.

She devoured him openly, like soil deprived of water,

unable to tear her gaze away since he'd been gone for a fortnight. Dark shadows hung under his slate-gray eyes. He'd obviously showered because his hair gleamed with raven-black wetness but strangely, he hadn't shaved yet. She knew he shaved twice a day and judging by the thick bristle covering his jaw, he'd missed more than once.

His lovely mouth was hidden and yet Ali liked him like this. He looked gruff and approachable and sexy. She could go on a discovery path, trailing her mouth over that bristle looking for the mouth that kissed so well. That tasted like heaven and heat.

His pale gray shirt was untucked and a couple of buttons were undone. When he stood up, she saw that he was wearing dark jeans and the denim molded enticingly to his hard thighs. Her mouth dried, and every promise she'd made to herself that she wouldn't moon over him like a lovesick teenager died an instant death.

"*Buongiorno*, Alisha."

Deep and husky, the sound of his voice was so good to hear. She'd desperately missed it and him. But seeing him when she couldn't touch him was just as bad an ache.

"I don't think I've ever seen you without a close shave," she said, her voice barely rising above a whisper. "Although the lumbersexual look works too."

Only when his brows raised and his eyes came alive with a fiery glint did she realize what she said. Heat filled her cheeks. "You surprised me. Izzy said you wouldn't be back until Sunday."

"I cut the trip short. I tried not to wake you last night."

"I heard you though, so—"

"So it's not really a surprise to see me this morning then, is it?" He had her there. "You look tired. Lovely but tired."

"I haven't been sleeping well. Been working a lot. How was Tokyo?"

"Same old stuff. Lots of meetings from dawn to dusk, then dinner, then more work. And few hours later, this morning, the same old fires again."

She'd never heard him sound so…dismissive of work before. Never seen him looking anything but perfectly put together in his Armani three-piece suits. Almost as if the power was a cloak he wore to hide the complex man beneath.

She frowned, even as she greedily swept her gaze over the way the tight denim clung to his thighs. She knew the power in those thighs, remembered how they'd clenched rock hard when she dug her nails in. "You're wearing jeans. And you didn't shave. It's nine thirty and you're still here. Your laptop is not even open." She rattled off one thing after the other, trying to arrest the pure longing coursing through her. "I know because I checked the time before I came out. I've been awake since five thirty and I took extra long in the shower because I know you don't leave until six thirty and I made sure that…"

"Made sure that you didn't come out until I left?"

His gaze held hers and all the air left her lungs. She licked her lips and a fierce fire awakened in his eyes.

The memory of what had happened between them that night charged the air. Her breasts ached for his hands, and wetness pooled between her thighs.

"Yes. I have a big day."

His elegantly long fingers stilled in the process of pouring coffee from the French press in his hands. The slosh of the liquid made him look down. He shook his fingers and pushed them under the tap. Ali didn't move even as she wanted to go to him. She would beg again, and she'd promised herself she wouldn't.

"There's burn cream under the sink," she offered.

He turned the tap off and looked sideways at her, his mouth twitching. "Are you not going to move from that spot?"

"I have to leave."

"Without your coffee first?" The teasing tone of his words, the way he was looking at her, Ali was terrified and ready to run. This was pure torment on so many levels.

"Where are you off to?"

She checked the platinum wristwatch—her mother's old watch that he'd found in her father's things and had had fixed for her. So many small things he had done for her. The camera, the studio, this watch…and yet he denied her with his words. "I'm meeting with that agent this afternoon."

He smiled and it lit up the entire room. "Good. That's good. Give me fifteen minutes to deal with something and I'll drive you."

Alarm bells went off in her head. And her body. The last thing she needed was continued exposure to him.

He was her kryptonite, he always would be. And wasn't that just pathetic?

"Why?"

"For moral support."

She glared at him. "Because you think my work is so bad that he'll automatically reject me?"

He raised his hands, palms up in an "I surrender" gesture. "Are you always going to twist my words and fight me for the rest of our lives?"

The rest of their lives…it was like a punch to her midriff. There was no rest of their lives, not if she wanted to be sane. Once she saw this agent, she would know what to focus on next. Her career at least would always provide an escape from London. And from him.

"You think you're not good enough—for your papa, for the charity, for the agent. For the world. Not me. You made that decision all by yourself."

"That's not true," she offered as a token protest, the depth of his perception stealing her breath.

He was right. Despite her mama's best efforts, she'd always wondered why her papa had given her up. Why Vikram had simply abandoned her.

Why her papa had never loved her like he did Vicky and Dante.

Why, why, why, why had she so easily assumed it was she that lacked something?

Not good enough for Dante either.

That was what she had thought that night at the mansion.

Why assume that Dante didn't want to be with her because she was not good enough?

Was that why she was ready to run away again instead of standing and fighting for the most real relationship she'd ever had in her life?

The questions came at her like missiles while he simply watched.

"Why do you want to come with me?" she said, going on the defensive. It was her one remaining coping mechanism. "When just a few weeks ago, you called it my fun hobby?"

"*Mia dispiace*, Ali. I was wrong about you on a lot of levels. I've seen you slog in the darkroom for hours on end. And I'm assuming at least some of it wasn't just to avoid me. *Si?*"

"*Si.* I've been working on this collection for a long time now and it's finally coming together. I develop my own prints and it's time-consuming."

Tenderness she'd never thought him capable of shone in his face. "Will you forgive me for mocking your passion? For—?"

"For being an arrogant jackass for as long as I've known you?" she added with a smile of her own.

His chin hit his chest in a mockery of remorse, his palm went to his breastbone and he glanced up at her through those long lashes that should have made him look feminine and instead made him stunningly gorgeous. She laughed out loud.

Who knew the man could be just as dramatic as her?

"*Si,* I forgive you. I… We were both wrong on many things. I didn't realize how many things we even have in common."

Like their ambition to prove themselves to the world, their loyalty and their love for her father and...

"Yeah? Like what?"

She blinked at the sudden intensity of his question. "Like our love of cheese. I mean, come on, that's a solid basis for a lifelong relationship." Her words drifted away onto a whisper as she realized what she was saying.

He didn't want a relationship with her.

Only her voting shares—no one could blame Dante for mind games at least. "It's not necessary. I've been doing things alone for a long time."

"I don't want that to be the case anymore. I want to come with you because I remember how nervous I was the first time Neel asked me to handle a client all on my own. I was—" he scrunched his brow and she wanted to kiss the line he got between his eyebrows when he did that "—twenty-three, twenty-four...and I was so determined to make a good impression that I almost sent out contracts with the wrong dates on them. I'd like to be there for you, Alisha."

"Because you owe it to Papa?" She folded her hands, hurt splintering through her. "This sympathy thing is getting old fast."

She got out nothing else for he covered the distance between them. The scent of him had her swaying toward him. She wanted to bury her face in his neck, she wanted to breathe him in until he was the only one in her world. "No. I'm not doing this for Neel. Or for the company. Or any*one* or any*thing*. I want to do it for you."

"Don't you have to work?" she said, his words weaving magic into her soul.

"I thought I'd take the day off. After your meeting, we can go out for lunch."

"Lunch? Dante, I told you, I don't want to—"

He bent and kissed her cheek and every molecule in Ali's body stilled. The contact was soft, tender, his beard a rough rasp in contrast. Her knees shook beneath her and she had no choice but to anchor her hands over his shoulders.

She felt the tremble that went through him as he wrapped his fingers around the nape of her neck. "I promise you, *bella mia*. Tonight we'll talk and if you still want to leave the flat, we'll discuss our options. But you can't just leave London." The emotion in his eyes was a hot burn against her skin, stealing away her protest. "I would never hurt you, Ali, you know that, *si*?"

Ali hid her face in his chest and nodded. Even knowing that, it wasn't in his hands. For all his good intentions, he would hurt her. Because he was becoming more and more important to her, no, *essential* to her and she had no way to stop that.

She was just about to pull away from him when the front door to the penthouse opened. They turned like that together, surprised, since security hadn't even called to announce the arrival of any visitors.

An older woman and a younger woman—the former clearly Dante's mother from the strong resemblance between them—walked in. The security guard placed a collection of designer luggage discreetly behind them and left with a nod at Dante.

Both women stared at the way she was half leaning into Dante, her body pressed into his side with his fingers around the nape of her neck. As if walking in on a married couple in an intimate embrace was a shocking sight.

For all they knew, she and Dante could have been having sex on the living room sofa or at the breakfast bar, or standing up against the back wall, or…

Coloring at how quickly her thoughts had gone in that direction, Ali tried to move away from Dante but his arm held her rigidly, his fingers digging into her hips. He relented a little when she gasped, but his arm stayed around her waist, pressing their sides together. He seemed oblivious to her discomfort as he stared at the woman standing behind his mother.

"*Buongiorno*, Dante," the striking beauty said, tilting her chin up in a silent challenge. A torrent of rapid-fire Italian fell from her mouth.

There was a thread of something, a possessiveness, an intimacy, that brought Ali's spine straight. She glanced between the woman who had to be Dante's age and Dante, who still looked at her as if he was seeing a ghost.

The woman had exquisite features, was dressed in the height of haute couture in a beige-colored pantsuit that clung to her voluptuous curves and looked as if she had just walked off the pages of a fashion magazine instead of a long flight.

A surge of something unpleasant rose in Ali's chest. Without thought, she covered Dante's fingers with her own. To pull him back to the present, she told herself.

The words rang hollow, even inside her own head. Good Lord, the last thing she was going to do was fight over him when he'd been clear about what he didn't want from her.

And it didn't look like he was even going to introduce her to his guests. Neither of the women so much as looked in her direction.

She went on her toes and said, "I'm going to leave while you...deal with them. Enjoy your day off." And since her mama had taught her manners, she smiled at the two women. "I'll see you later."

His fingers fanned around over her hip as he pulled her even closer. The press of his chest against hers made her breathless. "I told you I'd drive you to the meeting." He bent and rubbed his nose against hers. "Don't run away, Alisha."

Her heart beat double time, a whisper of hope and joy threading through her.

The other woman spoke again, in Italian, something to the effect of she'd been looking forward to seeing Dante or spending time with Dante. Ali frowned. "Are you doing this for...her sake?"

He scowled. "What?"

"Did you take the day off for them?"

"I had no idea my mother was on a flight to London." When that melodious voice piped up again, he cut her short with one look. "Ali doesn't understand Italian. Please speak in English, Francesca."

Francesca's smile dimmed at the edges as she nodded at Ali, as if she were the bloody queen of England granting a peasant a great honor. "Hello, Alisha."

"Hi, Francesca."

"Aren't you going to welcome us, Dante?" Sylvia Ferramo asked.

Ali knew very little about his mother, even for all the sensational coverage of his father's crime all those years ago. Sylvia looked no older than forty-five at the most. There was a delicacy to her expression, a fragility to the bones of her face as if she would break at the lightest whiff of air.

Finally, Dante addressed his mother. "Since you decided to take the trip *without* informing me, Mama," he stressed and the woman colored, and the tight grip on Ali's heart released, "I'm sure you do not require me to invite you in. You can breakfast with us and shower if you'd like. I'll ask my assistant to book you a suite at Four Seasons."

"No," Sylvia said, walking in and reaching for his hands. "I'm seeing my son after a long time, *si*?" One arm still around Ali's waist, Dante bent only after she tugged at him so that she could kiss his cheeks. He offered no embrace and even worse, he radiated a brooding tension that clearly discouraged her from coming closer. "Francesca and I will not mind sharing a room here. Our visit is short and I, especially, want to see more of you than I would at some luxury hotel."

He still said nothing. Ali had never seen him so shocked, or so intentionally rude. Hoping to cover up the protracted silence, she offered her hand to Sylvia. "Hello, Mrs. Ferramo. Please, stay for as long as you like. I'm gone for most of the day anyway and in fact, if it gets too tight here, I can just bunk out on the sofa in my studio on the forty-eighth floor."

"You're not going anywhere," Dante commanded, just as Sylvia shook her hand.

Though there was no warmth in her eyes, her smile was polite and open. She examined Ali as if she were a foreign insect. As if she could weigh just from one look whether Ali was good enough for her son. "I was quite surprised to read about your wedding in the news. I have no idea why my son chose to hide his bride from me. Or why it all happened so quickly."

This time, there was no mistaking the implied innuendo in her words. "Mama, if you want to spend time with my wife and me, without being invited in the first place, then you will at least be civil. You'll keep your numerous innuendos and suggestions and caustic remarks to yourself. Alisha is mine to protect and I will not tolerate the kind of poison you're so good at spreading here, capisce?"

Mine to protect. Her heart crawled into her throat.

Her cheeks paling, Sylvia nodded.

"Now let me show you to your rooms."

Feeling like a fourth wheel who didn't understand the undercurrents, Ali picked up her handbag and portfolio from the sitting lounge. The coffee would be cold now anyway. She didn't miss the longing, doe-eyed look Francesca cast Dante either. The woman had come with the express purpose of renewing a friendship, even knowing that Dante had a wife of barely a month.

Maybe because Dante had told her how it was between them?

She came out into the foyer and pressed the button to call the elevator. This was good. Francesca and his mother were exactly what she needed until she figured out her next step.

"Where are you going?" Dante said right behind her, and before she could respond, he took her portfolio from her. "I told you I'd take you to the meeting. And before you ask again, for God's sake, I didn't invite my mother, or Francesca."

"So, is she the blast from your past?"

"What?"

Very much not the question she needed to ask. "Never mind. It's not my business."

Holding her gaze, he put her portfolio down with the utmost care and then advanced on her. Like a frightened rabbit, Ali stepped back until her bottom hit the back wall. Leaning forward, he caged her on all sides. He was all over her and yet he wasn't touching her at all. "Ask me, Ali. Anything."

She wanted to ask him why he was so cold toward his mother, or why he never mentioned her. Or why she'd not been a part of his life for all these years. Why a man who'd been so devoted to her father, who'd grieved Vikram and who cared about Ali, didn't care about his own family.

Instead, she asked the question she knew would devour her for the rest of the day. "Who is she?"

"The girl I wanted to marry a long time ago. She broke it off and, with hindsight, I'm glad she did. And she's firmly in the past."

"So that…thing between me and you back there was petty revenge?"

"Nessuno." The foyer rang with his denial. "I would never, never use you like that."

"Then what was it?" She closed her eyes. Their relationship was like a minefield—so many unexploded and untouchable subjects. But one touch and the passion between them ignited. One step and their bodies would connect and it would be heaven and she was shaking for the effort it took to hold herself back. "Don't play games with me, Dante. I'm not as strong as you think."

"I think you're the strongest, bravest, the most beautiful woman I've ever known." His breath caressed her cheek, sending sparks swooping down her skin. "Ali?"

"Hmm?"

"Don't you want to wait until tonight to know?"

She opened her eyes and as she saw her reflection in his gray eyes, Ali knew. It was too late for her. "Know what?"

With each word, he moved closer, until his nose was buried in her neck. Until she felt the tension swathing his powerful frame. Until he was everything, her entire world. "I want this…us to be real." He lifted her left hand and stared at her bare finger. "I…want you never to take off your rings again. I want to take you to bed and stay there for a month. I want your loyalty and your fidelity. I want you to be my true wife."

"And what do I get?" she whispered automatically, mesmerized by the intensity of his expression, unable to kill the hope fluttering in her chest.

To belong to Dante, to be his in every way…

He smiled then and it was a thing of wicked beauty. "I never intended to marry, you know. After the thing between Francesca and me. Never. But you… I don't think I can go another day without making you mine. You will have everything I have to give. My fortune at your feet, my body and my fidelity. It'll be my privilege to call you my wife, my privilege to take care of you, my privilege to give you all the pleasure you could ever want."

Not love. Everything but love.

She knew him well and she knew that he hadn't left the word out on purpose. For a man who'd never meant to marry, for a man who had a long-standing mistress in Matta Steel, of course, love wasn't a priority.

Love wasn't even in his thoughts.

He hadn't said he wouldn't love her either. God, was she clutching at straws?

He touched his forehead to hers and let out a long exhale. "Say yes, Alisha, and you'll never be alone again. You'll never want for anything."

Before those words could sink in, before her world could tilt back to its right axis, he pulled away. His gorgeous eyes shimmered with desire, his hands tucked into his trouser pockets pulled at the front, calling her gaze to his arousal.

A soft sound fell from her mouth as desire hit her hard and fast. She fisted her hands, fighting the urge to trace the shape of him, the urge to beg him to take her here, in the foyer, while his mother was in the next room.

"*No.* Don't take another step. Be my wife and I'm all yours."

Ali cursed as even now he denied himself and her.

"This is the only way this is going to happen." He ran his palm over his jaw, devouring her with his gaze, his shoulders tight. "In fact, I'm shocked at how long it took me to realize how perfect you and I will be. I'd like to think even Neel would have approved. I want you and I like you and I want to protect you. We know each other. The fire we have…is no common thing. Together, we can build a good marriage based on respect and a bond that will never break. Together, we'll be his legacy."

She spoke through panic, from the same desire running fierce in her veins. "If you say marrying me is paying his debt to you, I'll never look at you again."

"No, *cara mia*. It's not a debt. But I'm a man with principles and as much as I want to be inside you right now, it won't happen. You are not any woman. You'll never be just any woman to me. Be my wife, Alisha, give me your vows truly. Promise me your commitment. There will be no cheap, dirty affair so that you can scratch an itch and run away when it suits you. Or when it gets hard. Or when it gets old.

"For once in your life, have the courage to stay.

"It has to be all the way between us, *tesoro*. All or nothing."

CHAPTER NINE

Come to me, Alisha.

DANTE'S TEXT FROM two hours ago drummed in her head as Ali finally rode the elevator to the penthouse. It wasn't lost on her that he hadn't explained his disappearance for most of the evening, with Francesca in tow, after stealing the ground from under her with his announcement.

He didn't say please.

He didn't cajole or persuade even.

He just commanded her as if she were his to command. As if there was no doubt she'd accept this. As if she was so desperate to be with him that she would simply breeze into being his wife.

And this was how their relationship would be too, she had no doubt. He might as well have said *Give me your heart and soul* outside the elevator earlier in the day.

Oh, but she desperately wanted to belong to him. Not because she'd spent her whole life looking for a place to belong. But because he was what she'd been searching for.

Because he was right, she was tired of running away. Of being scared.

She wanted to stay and fight for him, for this, for them.

But incensed by his arrogance, she'd texted back.

Say plz.

His silence for almost a half hour had killed her. She'd just stared at her phone waiting, watching, desperately yearning.

Sitting in the quiet blackness of her darkroom, the *ping-ping-ping* of her cell phone had set her heart thundering in her ears. Her fingers shaking, she'd looked at the texts.

Just "please", cara mia? Come to me and I'll go down on my knees for you.

You're mine, Alisha. So stop playing games.

Take one step toward me and I'll give you heaven.

The possessiveness, the promise, the passion… She had trembled at the picture he painted, laughed at how, even in his texts, he was so…*Dante*.

Because what he did give was absolute. It was in his actions, it was in the way he gave everything to her father's legacy and it was in the way he cared about his employees. In the way he'd gotten to the core of her in mere weeks. In the way he'd prodded and pushed her into being her best.

She could tour the world another decade and she'd never find a man like Dante.

So there she was, standing outside his bedroom door while her future waited on the other side. The rectangle of light peeking from under the door made her pulse dizzy. It was half past one in the night and finally, thankfully, the flat was silent.

Of course, Ali could never forget the fact that Sylvia and Francesca were just a few doors down, after refusing again his offer that they'd be more comfortable at the Four Seasons. For her part, Sylvia seemed desperate to make a connection with Dante and Ali couldn't begrudge her that.

She'd give anything to see her papa or Vikram just one more time and say sorry for all the hurtful things she'd done. But Dante's ex was another matter altogether.

Ali had ended up going alone to the meeting with the agent. Because something had blown up with the Japanese merger and Dante had had to leave. She hadn't pinned her hopes on him coming and yet she'd been disappointed.

She'd been waiting on tenterhooks most of the evening for Dante and Francesca to return from some urgent meeting. During dinner, Sylvia having grilled Ali enough to last a lifetime, about Papa and Vikram and their wedding, he hadn't offered any more info on the big secret meeting.

Now here she was, outside his door, her heart battering against her rib cage. But if she didn't go in, she'd never forgive herself for chickening out, for not even giving them a chance.

Gathering a long breath, she twisted the knob, walked in and closed the door behind her.

He was sitting at his desk, the lamp playing with the planes and hollows of his face. He was still in his white dress shirt, unbuttoned all the way now, and black trousers. His hair stood out at all angles, making even more of his high forehead and the slashes of his cheekbones.

The air around him thrummed with palpable tension, and Ali saw there was nothing in front of him on the desk except the phone.

She hadn't texted back after his messages, which had been a half hour ago. And as he stared at her, she saw in his face the same desperation she felt, the taut need, the uncertainty in the tight line of his mouth.

His gaze swept over her from top to bottom—from her hair in that messy topknot to the tight stretchy sweater dress.

She leaned against the door, digging her nails into the wood grain. "Did you think I wouldn't come?"

He shrugged and the action parted his shirt wider, giving her a peek of his defined pectorals with flat brown nipples and tight abdominal muscles. She licked her lips, imagining running her tongue against that rock-hard band.

He made a low, growling sound that went straight to her sex.

"Tell me."

"I wasn't sure you'd come." He ran his hand through his hair as if the admission cost him.

She thought it would make her feel better, less vulnerable to see that he hadn't been sure of her. She didn't.

Suddenly, she wasn't interested in power games with him. Not anymore. "Why didn't you come to me then? Why this mind-play?" A raw vulnerability filled her, coating her throat with tears. She wanted him so much. She ached to be held by him, she longed to belong to him.

"Isn't it enough that I've been yours for the taking from that first evening in Bangkok? Enough that I came back to the flat against every rational instinct? Enough that I waited all evening, after you disappeared for the evening with your ex?

"What do I have to do—crawl to you on my knees to make you understand that this isn't just an itch? That this is not a phase or a stopgap or a…"

He pushed off from the desk, reaching her before she could blink. His hand went around her neck, pulling her to him. His mouth took hers in such a roughly erotic kiss that her throat dried, her breath stuttered, her belly swooped. She gasped and he swooped into her mouth with a mastery that made her sex clench and throb.

"It had to be your choice, Alisha. Do you not see, *bella mia*? This is far too important to me. This is…" he whispered against her mouth, his gaze so intense that she felt stripped to the bone. "This can't be some boardroom deal where I use your weakness against you to make you surrender. This can't be a taking. I needed you to come to me, to choose this on those conditions."

He clasped her cheeks and peppered kisses all over her face, a desperate intensity in his words. "This is the first time in my life I've waited, and wanted, not knowing what the outcome would be. But now that you're here, *cara mia*, you'll never have to take that step again.

"I'll forever cherish what you give me. You've undone me, *tesoro*."

His teeth bit, his tongue stroked, his body pressed her against the wall until every inch of his hard body was plastered against hers. His unrelenting chest crushed her breasts. His lips—God, his lips—nipped and rubbed until Ali was nothing but a quivering mass of sensations. Until hunger for more consumed her.

His deep groan soothed and excited at the same time. And then his tongue was inside her mouth again, laving at her with rough, long strokes. She stroked hers against his and then sucked on it. His arms around her tightened, one hard thigh wedging between hers.

Hardness and heat, he was hers. Tremors swept through her.

His mouth moved to her jaw. He licked her earlobe before his teeth bit down on the tender flesh. Ali jerked and rubbed her core against his thigh.

"Wait," he said, jolting his lower body away from her, his glorious chest falling and rising. "Francesca… her ex pumped all her money into some get-rich scheme and she came here for my help."

"She came here for more than that, believe me."

"We spent all evening with my team of lawyers and PIs to figure out how to help her. And I did it tonight because I want her out of here as soon as possible. Whatever she and Mama thought about coming here, I have no interest in her." He took her hand up to his mouth and kissed her palm. "You're my wife and tell me you believe me that I'll never look at another woman like that again. My word means everything to me."

Ali nodded, feeling a catch in her throat.

He gathered her into his arms, his forehead brushing hers. And sighed. "Tonight is your lucky night, *cara mia*."

"Why just me?" She dug her teeth into his chin and he jerked. "I'm a good lay too, you know. If you want proof—"

He tugged at her hair roughly, thrusting his tongue in, murmuring something in Italian that she was pretty sure meant her mouth was going to get her into a lot of trouble. Or that he was going to shut her up the only way he knew.

He was hot, rough, thrusting in and out with his tongue. His hands moved compulsively over her back, her waist, coming to rest on her buttocks. In a rough movement that betrayed his lack of control, he pulled her up until his erection pressed up against the V of her legs. Their groans rent the air, the hard ridge of his shaft a perfect fit against her soft core. "I forgot to buy condoms." His hands snuck under her top and her belly clenched at the rough contact of his palm. "So, it's all you tonight."

Ali shivered at the wickedness in his tone. "As exciting as that sounds, why do you not have condoms here?"

"I don't bring lovers here. You're the first woman who's lived in this flat, who's come into my room and who's going to share my bed."

"That makes me feel special," she said flippantly. Because flippancy had always been her default response when she was protecting herself from hurt.

"You think I do this lightly?"

Ali shook her head. The one thing she'd never doubt was Dante's word, his commitment once he gave it. "Two lovers. I'm clean and I'm on the pill."

His eyes took on a thunderous look, as if he didn't like hearing that. He rubbed his jaw, and studied her. "Five. I'm clean."

That unpleasant feeling gripped her and she tried to chase it away. He was hers now. "Five? Maybe you forgot how to count because I can recount off the top—"

"Rumors and gossip? I took Matta Steel to a net worth of five billion dollars in ten years. I don't have time to have as many affairs as the media hints."

"Is…Francesca one of those five?"

The shutters that fell down in his eyes were instant. He let her go and Ali missed his warmth like a limb. "Let it go."

"How would you feel if Jai was in the flat, two doors down?"

"I'd throw him out by the scruff of his collar."

"Even though I repeatedly told you he was out of my life?"

He rubbed his face again. "This will never work if we don't trust each other."

"I do trust you. It's just that…you know everything about me. All my weaknesses. I know nothing about you."

"You haven't let me see your work."

"So earn that right, Dante."

"Francesca's parents broke off our association the minute the news of my father's crime came out. We'd been together for most of our lives. When I asked her about her parents' decision, she said she was abiding by it. She didn't want to marry a man whose father's crime would always cling to him. Who owed millions to people, who could never leave that infamy behind."

"She broke your heart."

He looked up and shook his head. "*No.* Funnily enough, by that time, I'd been dealt much worse."

Maybe Francesca hadn't broken his heart but she'd made him close himself off. Ali went to him, hating the distance he put between them. "I'm glad then that she has such a fickle heart. Because now you're mine.

"One woman's discard is another woman's hero."

A white smile flashed in his dark face, lust turning his eyes impossibly darker. "I'm no hero, Ali. Heroes don't exist, *cara mia.* Only men with weaknesses and men without."

She didn't like the gravity of his tone. The shadow of his father's dark past was in his eyes. Twining her arms around his neck, she rubbed herself against him shamelessly. His erection was a brand against her belly. "Fine, you're no hero. You're the perfect man with the perfect hard-on and I can't wait—"

He tucked a swath of hair behind her ear. "I need to learn what turns you on. I need to make you scream. I need to lick every inch of you. Then, if you're still willing, then I will be inside you, *cara mia.*"

Heat scoured her cheeks and Ali tugged her gaze

down to his neck. "Oh, God, you're going to be all me-thodical and in control, aren't you?"

His laughter surrounded her even as his words wound anticipation tighter and tighter inside her. She snuck her fingers into his hair, pushing away the thick lock that fell onto his forehead. He looked down at her and smiled and in that smile, Ali found the entire world. The thing that she'd been searching for through the years and continents—a place to belong. A place to call her own.

This man was worth staying still for. Worth fight-ing for.

It felt as if she'd been waiting her whole life for this moment. With this man. Every choice she'd made had led her here. To tonight.

To Dante.

Dante moved away from Ali. Every muscle in him curled tight with a hunger he couldn't deny anymore.

It felt right. All the way to his bones.

Her soft voice, full of vulnerability tugged at him. Reaching for the wall behind him, he turned on the overhead ceiling lights and the room was instantly ablaze. And in the middle of the room, leaning against his king bed, stood Alisha.

The cashmere dress she wore hugged every swell and dip of her body, the peach tone setting off her dusky skin. The dress ended inches above her knees, while her legs were clad in knee-high brown boots, leaving miles of toned thighs on display. Her breasts jutted up high and firm and he knew, just knew, that she wasn't wearing a bra.

After years of self-discipline and having sex for the simple release it provided, tonight he wanted to gorge on her.

Now that she was here, he wanted to take his time. He wanted her limp and damp and blown apart. He wanted to drown her in so much pleasure that she'd forget any other man's name. He never wanted her to feel as if she'd made a compromise with him. She would never want for anything as his wife. Not for riches, not for security and not for pleasure.

He ran a hand over his jaw, feeling the scratch of his stubble. "Stay there while I shave. I won't be long."

"No, don't." The tip of her tongue swept over her lush lower lip and he felt that hesitant stroke lower on his body. The very thought of her hands on his shaft, that tongue wrapped around his hardness sent him to the very edge he'd talked himself away from just now.

"No?" he said, raising a brow. Silky, hoarse, his voice sounded so unlike him. "Tell me why not."

"I…I like your stubble."

He had no idea how he managed to stay still, all the way across the room. How he managed to hang on to the last thread of his control when all he wanted was to splay her legs wide and pound into her. "Why?"

She tucked her hand into the cowl-neck of her sweater dress, as if she found her very skin restless. As if she couldn't wait to shed it all. "I want to feel it against my skin."

Desire slammed into him anew, a fever in his blood. "Where, Ali?"

She lifted her chin, his equal every step of the way. "Here." She rubbed her cheek. "Here." Her pink-tipped fingers rubbed the nipple poking against the dress. "Here." Her palm swooped down over her belly. "And here." Now her palm was between her thighs.

His mouth dried out. "Pull your hair down."

Hands raised into that mass, she pulled at the clip and it all came tumbling down in glorious, silky brown waves that framed her lovely face. And then she shook her head in that classic feminine gesture that drew his balls tight. He wanted to feel that hair on his belly and lower, he was going to fist his hands in that heavy mass and hold her still for him while he thrust into her wet heat.

Cristo, there were a thousand things he wanted to do to her. Inside her. With her. An eternity wouldn't be enough for all of it. "You'll feel it, *tesoro*, against your skin." He let his gaze rest on the jut of her breasts, her flat belly, to her thighs. "Everywhere."

Brown eyes widened into deep pools, and a soft mewl fell from her mouth. "Any other requests from my sexy wife?"

"Take your shirt off," she commanded him, in a tone that thrummed over his skin.

He shrugged it off his shoulders. It fluttered to the floor in a whisper. Her gaze moved over him hungrily, from his throat to his shoulders to his nipples, to the light sprinkling of hair on his chest, and then to the line of it that disappeared into his jeans.

And then strayed over the bulge in his pants.

Again, her tongue came out and licked her lower lip. His shaft lengthened, almost painfully hard now.

"Take that dress off," he said, struggling and failing to remove the rough need in his words. "Leave your boots on."

Her gaze gleamed. His breath hung on a jagged edge when she picked up the hem and pulled it over her head. Lust slammed into him like the side of a mountain. A growl escaped his throat—half pain, half pleasure at the breathtaking sensuality of her body.

She wasn't wearing a bra. Her breasts were small and high and round, the brown nipples puckered into tight knots. His mouth watered. Miles of smooth brown skin shimmered flawlessly under the bright lights. Silky hair fluttered over one side of her shoulder, beckoning his touch.

Her chest curved sharply into a narrow waist, small enough for him to wrap his hands around and flared into wide hips, followed by long, shapely thighs and legs, legs he wanted wrapped around him while he plunged into her.

Dios mio, she was a red-blooded male's wet dream. And she was his.

Only his, forever. This night and all the nights to come.

"Now the panties." His command rolled out of a dry mouth.

He thought she would refuse him, on principle. She'd always hated that he ordered her around, that he knew what was best for her.

"No arguments?" he said, goading her, wanting her to fight him. Needing something to fracture that utter surrender in her eyes. In her body.

"I've no problem following your commands when I know you have my best interests at heart."

A shudder went through him at the arrogant confidence in her voice, the husky timbre of it. Chin tilted up defiantly, gaze burning bright, she tucked her fingers into the thin seam of her panties and rolled them down.

She had to lean back against the bed to pull them over her boots and her hair fell forward like a silky curtain, covering her breasts from his view.

Skin clammy with need, he took her in, as she threw the panties at him, a wicked smile curving her mouth. The fabric fell to the ground as he moistened his lips.

His gaze went from her flat belly to the V of her pelvis, down to the black curls hiding her sex from him. She was gloriously sexy.

He shook with the need to just take her right there, standing like that, her eyes wide and swimming in desire. But not tonight. He would do that another night. He would take her without preamble, he would reach for her one night, kiss her awake slowly and she would welcome him and he would be inside her while they were laughing with each other, in the kitchen, in the living room, in the shower.

But tonight, he intended to take it slow if it killed him. He sat down on the leather recliner. "Come here to me," he growled out, patting his lap.

And she did, her hips swinging with each step, her breasts swaying up and down, her mouth curved in a teasing light. She came over to him with such naked want in her eyes that his erection pushed against his trousers. When she stilled in front of him, her knees hitting the recliner, he leaned forward. His hands filled with her buttocks, he pressed her forward into his face. The scent of her arousal seeped into him like a drug. He shook from the force of his desire. He licked around her navel, breathing her in.

He left his trousers zipped, for he needed every ounce of control he had to bring her to climax first. For the first time in his life, Dante had nothing left because Ali had undone him.

Simply by giving him everything she had with such trust. Such open affection. Such…

It was a gift, he knew, and he promised himself he'd cherish it even if he couldn't return it in full measure.

"Climb into my lap. And straddle me."

Ali barely heard, much less understood Dante's words beneath the rushing in her ears. Knees shaking like Jell-O, she climbed up onto the recliner, while his hands traveled over every inch of her bare skin.

Cupping her buttocks, smoothing over her hips, tracing her rib cage, palming her breasts, then sweeping between her inner thighs without really touching her where she needed to be touched. Next they were at her back, pushing her down and forward. She sank into his lap and the feel of his hard shaft against her sex was like electricity in her veins.

Instantly, mindlessly, she moved over him and his growl ripped through the air. Rough hands gripped her hips, staying her. "Don't move, not yet. I want to come inside you."

"Yes. Please," she whispered on a dry mouth.

He tongued her nipple. A wet lash. Her back arched into the hot caress. Murmuring in Italian, he repeated the soft flicks of his tongue over and over again, until she was panting. Sobbing. Shaking. She dug her fingers into his thick hair and held his head to her breast, demanding more. Needing more. His teeth nipped before he closed his lips over the peak. "Every night after that time, I dreamed of this." He rolled her nipple in his mouth, pressed his tongue against it again and again before he sucked on it.

Fire burst through her belly.

Sensations poured over her like warm honey, beating on her, sending arrows of shooting pleasure down to her lower belly. And just when she was at the edge of mindless ecstasy, when she could taste the pleasure on her tongue like bottled lightning, he stopped.

Made her come down from the edge.

He repeated the torment again and again, until her skin was clammy with sweat. Her thigh muscles were trembling. And she was shaking with need. She looked down into his dark eyes. "You want me to beg, don't you? This is payback for all the trouble I caused you all these years?"

Rough hands stroked her bare back, down the line of her spine to her buttocks, up and down soothing her. He pressed a fierce kiss to her mouth, tongue and teeth whipping her into a frenzy again. His hand shook as he pushed back damp hair from her forehead, desire and something else in his eyes. "I like seeing you like that. Desperate for me. My name on your lips like a chant. Your eyes hazy and clouded. Your body so achingly gorgeous and mine to play with. It's like a drug, *cara mia*. Building you up, seeing you crave me like that... You give of yourself so boldly, so completely, so...generously. I promised myself I would have you limp and screaming my name for hours." Huskiness filled his words.

She rocked into him, craving his hardness at the apex of her thighs, delirious with need. Mindless for his possession. "Inside me, Dante, now, please."

He lifted her onto her knees. The rasp of his zipper, the sliding whisper of his jeans were havoc on her skin. His erection released up toward his belly, thick and long with veins she wanted to trace with her tongue. She licked her dry lips, and he growled. "Not tonight, *cara mia*."

Ali shook with violent need when he took himself in hand. "Lower yourself, slowly."

She lowered her hips and he rubbed the length of him against her wet folds. Pleasure knotted in her pelvis and she jerked at the overwhelming sensation.

His dark gaze stayed where he could see their bodies straining to join. "Do it again," he commanded and she did.

Once more, again and again, she pressed the plump head against her clit. And the next time she did it, he thrust his hips and he was inside her.

Ali gasped at how embedded he was inside her like this, stretching her to the hilt.

Sweat beaded on his forehead, the thick corded muscles of his neck standing out in stark relief. "*Maledizione*, you're so tight."

"It's been a long time. And now I know why I didn't even miss it. I was waiting for you, Dante."

A stillness came over him. "Ali, I don't deserve—"

"Shh…" she whispered and took his mouth in a soft kiss.

Stiff at first, slowly he melted into it as she tangled with his tongue just the way he liked. She ran her hands all over his warm, damp skin, loving the tight clench of his shoulders, the taut skin stretched over his chest. "You know, Jai was right. I didn't realize it for so long."

He scowled and cursed.

She wrapped her arms around him, loving the warmth and hardness of him surrounding her. "I've always had a thing for you. I've always weighed every man I meet against you. I don't even know when…"

His hands in her hair jerked her head back roughly. His nostrils flared and he rotated and thrust his hips at the same time. His thumb found her clit and pressed. On and on he worked her, with his shaft inside her, his fingers on her clit, as if he meant to make her mindless. And without warning, Ali came, liquid lightning splintering through her belly and lower.

His dark gaze devouring her, he kept thrusting, and the waves came and came, drowning her, dragging her.

She fell onto him, moaning, chasing the high still. "When what, Alisha?" he demanded, a craven starkness in his voice. "When what?"

"I don't know when it happened. Or maybe it was already there and it's only that I just see it now."

He stood up with their bodies still joined, his hands on her buttocks and he brought them to his bed. Pleasure began fluttering through her pelvis again when he kept her at the edge of the bed and started moving inside her.

There was an angry glint in his eyes, color burning beneath those cheekbones. The tenor of his thrusts quickened, his fingers painfully digging into her hips. She loved it, she loved that he was selfishly chasing his climax, that he wasn't clad in that cloak of control.

Ali pulled herself up on her elbows and met his mouth. "For years, it was easy to hide behind my hate." She dug her teeth into his lower lip and pulled. And in reward, his hips flexed and rotated.

Feral want painted his features with a harshness. His shoulders stood out in stark relief, a tremor in his skin when she claimed every part of him.

His nostrils flared as he dragged her even closer, pushing her thighs indecently wide with his shoulders.

He was glorious and she was the only one who could give him what he needed. She locked her legs at his buttocks and gave herself over to his rhythm.

Sweat beaded on his throat and then he pistoned once, twice, thrice, with a jerking motion. A growl fell from his mouth as he came—an uncontrolled, raw sound. She licked the sweat at his neck and bit his shoulder hard. "I love the sound you make when you come undone. I love how you know me so well. I love you, Dante. I'll always love you."

Smiling, Ali fell back against the sheets, her pelvis sore from the pounding, from the way he'd used her, her thighs trembling and aching. Her heart was so overflowingly full. He'd lost control there at the end because of what she'd said. And she reveled in it even as he remained silent. Even if every second of that silence pierced her.

She closed her eyes and turned her head away.

But not before she saw the shock in his eyes. And the stillness that came over him. And the way his entire body shuddered, his chin jerking as if she'd somehow dealt him a lethal blow.

For once, she didn't care what he was going through.

She was in love with him and there was a certain freedom in admitting that. In saying that out loud. In flinging her heart wide open and embracing what she felt.

In lying, satiated, next to the man she loved.

CHAPTER TEN

PINK DAWN WAS sweeping its fingers through the sky outside his bedroom, the world, the city pulsing into life as Dante came awake. For the first time in his life, he felt no rush to meet it. No urgent meeting, no PR emergency could wrench him away from the warm bed, the haven of his room, from Ali.

Two short weeks into his relationship with Ali, their true beginning, and it seemed like it had been two lifetimes. The first couple of days, he'd braced himself for some…flash of reality maybe, something to make him pay for the out-of-body experience he'd had with her that first night.

He kept expecting her to demand something, anything, in return for the declaration she'd made so boldly, so brazenly, so unflinchingly.

After all, he had countless memories of his mother declaring her love for his father, and then demanding a gift. A more expensive car, a diamond bracelet, a better flat…as if her love was a transaction. As if no word or deed was ever enough.

And his father, falling deeper and deeper, had never

realized that whatever he did would never be enough for her.

A knot formed in his stomach every time Ali kissed him, or laughed at him, or just plain looked at him. An expectant bracing to see what she would ask of him. Of what she'd demand that he couldn't give in the name of love.

It would be an awkward conversation, a hurtful one, but he'd been prepared to have it. She also seemed to have no expectation of hearing him return her declaration.

Because he couldn't love her. There was no force on earth that could propel him to open himself up to that kind of vulnerability, that kind of weakness, no way he would give her that power over him.

But she asked nothing of him, except his body. She was insatiable, just as much as he was and every night she came to him with that same naked desire in her eyes. She explored his body as if he was a sumptuous buffet she intended to gorge on, with her mouth, tongue, fingers.

She demanded her pleasure from him and took such effervescent delight in his pleasure, in seeking and discovering new ways to break his control, to bring him to his knees.

She asked nothing of him except his laughter, his company, his opinions. She didn't seem to have a plan beyond giving herself to him and simply expecting him to enjoy being with her. It was as if she'd reached through the fortress he'd built around his emotions and he found himself opening up.

This wasn't a transaction to her. Her love, or even her admission of it didn't demand a price.

She just gave. It just was.

I love you, Dante.

He couldn't tell himself it was from the sexual high she was floating on for he had never seen such clarity in her eyes. Such courage.

It had been like looking at the sun. He'd never thought giving could be as powerful as taking. And yet Ali managed to do just that, with him.

No, she had gazed into his eyes, both vulnerability and boldness in the tilt of her chin, her body thrusting up toward him, matching his hunger with hers, milking his shaft with her heat, her mouth against his chest, his heart thundering away under her touch, aching endlessly, craving more and more. She whispered those words like a benediction. Like a promise.

Just the memory of her was enough to send blood pooling in his groin, for that thrum to fill his blood. The sheet tented in front of him and he reached out a hand for her.

Cold, empty sheets greeted his hand. He frowned just as he heard the continuous *click-click* of a high-speed camera. With a curse, he sat up in the bed.

Dressed in a sleeveless T-shirt that stuck to her breasts and pink panties with cute bows on the sides, she was switching on the overhead lights. Dante blinked as bright light pierced his eyes. "Turn off the lights, *cara mia*. And come to bed."

She didn't answer. The sound of the shots she took pinged over his skin.

"Sit up for me, won't you, Dante? Please."

He sat up, almost unconsciously, the command in her voice driving his movements. She sounded nothing like the Ali he knew. "Push your hand through your hair."

Again, he found himself doing it before muttering, "I'm no model, Ali."

She dug her teeth into her lower lip, a frown on her face. "You're the sexiest man I've ever photographed and believe me, I've shot attractive men before."

"Naked?" he asked, possessiveness and something much baser filling his chest.

"*Si*, naked. Raise your arm, *por favor, caro mio*. I want the birthmark under your bicep in the shot. It's the only imperfection I've found so far in your body."

He smiled, the cajoling tone of her washing away anything else, the heat of the memory when she'd traced that and the small mole on his right thigh with her tongue filling his veins. "Make me a deal I can't refuse."

Warmth flushed her cheeks as she lowered the camera for the first time since he'd woken up. A wicked smile curved her lips. "I'll go down on you."

His erection twitched under the sheets and she licked her lips. He groaned.

"Altro," he said, knowing there was nothing in the world he would refuse her.

"You always ask for more," she pouted. "I'll let you go down on me."

As bold as she'd been the first night, it seemed there were depths to Alisha he would never learn. Hiding her face in his chest, she'd confided one night that her experiences had been few and not really of the adventurous type.

He let his gaze run down her belly to the V of her thighs, the pink silk barely covering her mound. His mouth watered at the very prospect of latching his lips over her sex, of thrusting his tongue into her tightness while she screamed his name. Of holding her down while she writhed under his mouth.

She clutched her thighs close as if she could hear his thoughts and he laughed. *"Altro."*

"I will let you see my work," she said softly. "But you have to promise me that you won't…that you will not… It's my heart and soul, Dante."

Warmth unlike anything he'd ever known spread through his chest. "It would be my honor to see your work. And my privilege to pose for you," he added and saw her smile widen, reach her eyes, and just like that, another layer of ice around his heart seemed to thaw.

That tension faded from his body. They would have the marriage he wanted. They would have everything together without the emotional transaction of love coloring every exchange.

"Okay, now, raise both your hands for me, please," she commanded and he happily played along.

A week later, Ali waved at Izzy as she passed her desk and without knocking, pushed open the door to Dante's office on the top floor of Matta Towers.

Standing against the far wall, with his back to her, he didn't hear her arrival. Ali took the time to study him, her heart pounding away. She'd never visited

Matta Towers, even when her papa had been alive, on principle.

Vikram had invited her, several times. She even remembered Dante inviting her once, going as far as saying that Neel would be happy to see her there. She, intent on cutting off her nose to spite her face, had refused. Because she'd been waiting for her papa to invite her.

Now, she would wait forever.

And she didn't want to let him make the same mistake.

His suite was vast with a stunning view of the London skyline, a dark mahogany desk, as imposing as the man himself, taking center stage. Creamy leather sofas sat in the small sitting area to the left, and to her right was another door through which she knew was his personal suite. Where he had probably been sleeping for the last three nights, because he certainly hadn't come home.

When she had called his cell phone and asked after the first night, he'd informed her, almost politely it had seemed, that the Japanese merger was taking all his time. Having heard of the passive-aggressive communication misfire her scheming uncle had taken part in, almost bringing the deal to a halt, she knew that he was telling her the truth. Not that she thought Dante would lie to her. If he was bored with her, or if that initial frenzy of desire they had both been drowning in receded, he would tell her.

She had a feeling it was to do with the frequent bouts of his mother's crying in the evenings, in the confronta-

tions she seemed determined to have, regardless of the
fact that it embarrassed Ali and infuriated Dante. Thank
goodness Francesca had left after the first few days.

But the wretchedness in Sylvia's eyes tore at Ali and
she couldn't just watch anymore.

"Dante?" she whispered, bracing herself for that con-
suming gaze.

He turned and just like that, pure longing filled her.
He looked sharp and arrogant as usual, but there were
dark shadows under his slate-gray eyes. Warmth flicked
into life in his tired eyes and her heart ached.

She thought he might ask her to come to him. Or he
would come to her, take her in his arms and kiss her
senseless. After all, it had been three days since he'd
touched her or kissed her or even held her. She missed
him like there was an ache in her chest.

But he did no such thing. The warmth of that smile
dimmed as he pushed his hands into his trouser pockets and leaned back against that wall.

In that moment, Ali realized something. He never
touched her outside the context of sex. As insatiable as
his passion was when he wanted her, he wasn't the de-
monstrative kind in public. But his stance clearly said
that she was interrupting. He confirmed it when he said,
"I have a meeting in fifteen minutes. Why didn't you
tell me you were coming all the way over? I would've
told you I was busy."

She swallowed, refusing to take his words as the
complete dismissal they were. He wasn't going to get
out of it that easily. This wasn't even about her, she reminded herself. It was about him.

And his mother and his past.

Brazening it out with a wide smile, she covered the distance between them. Before he could push her away, she went on tiptoes and kissed his mouth softly. Slowly. Pouring all the love in her heart into the kiss. For all the hardness of his body, she was amazed how soft his lips were, and for all his dismissive words, how he let her do what she wanted.

She traced the sharp angles of his face with her mouth—the blade of his nose, the high planes of his cheekbones, the hollows of his cheeks, his tight brow. Sinking her fingers into his crisp hair, she tugged and pulled. He came to her, willingly, giving in. She traced her way down to his neck, licked his pulse, pressed her tongue into the hollow of his neck. The familiar taste of skin, the scent of him calmed the furor in her blood. "Didn't anyone ever teach you that was the proper way to greet your wife after not seeing her for three days?"

After what seemed an eternity, the stiffness left his shoulders. A familiar shudder went through him. He pushed off from the wall with a soft growl, his hands sinking into her hair. "No, this is how I would greet my wife," he said, and bit hard into her lower lip. When she gasped at the pain-pleasure, he licked the hurt away. He took over the kiss with utter possession that sent currents arrowing toward her sex.

Wet, warm and wanton, she clung to him for breath, clinging to him for everything he could give. Hands around his shoulders, Ali rubbed herself against him mindlessly, desperate for more. His hands were at her buttocks again, his mouth at her neck. "I'll ask Izzy to postpone the meeting for another half hour. I need to be inside you, now."

She had no idea how she found the strength to say no; to pull away when all she wanted was to feel him inside her, to feel the closeness he allowed only during sex, to feel as if everything in her world was right again. "No, Dante, I didn't come here to have sex."

He released her so fast that she'd have fallen back if not for his swift reflex. His chest rose and fell, his mouth narrowed. Eyes glittering, he rubbed the back of his hand over his mouth. As if he wanted to wipe her taste away. "Then what was the point of the kiss, *cara mia*? To prove that you can fell me to my knees in a matter of a few minutes?"

She flinched at the soft cruelty of his words.

"I wasn't aware that we're supposed to keep track of who breaks whom. I never... I kissed you because I missed you. And that turned into something else, because it always does when we kiss. Or have you been sleepwalking through the last few weeks?"

Color washed over his cheeks. "I...I don't have time for this. Go home, Alisha."

He never called her Alisha like that anymore, the very word dripping with contempt and exaggerated patience. As if she was being purposely troublesome.

Which in itself was a clear sign that he wasn't all right. A month ago, she was sure he wouldn't have lost his temper like that with her. But neither was she going to think of his nasty words as some sort of progress between them.

She folded her hands, the hurt cycling to anger. "But

you have time to have a quickie with me against the wall? And after? You'll make me clean myself up in the bathroom and send me home with a pat and some cash?"

The curse that fell from his mouth sounded downright filthy. He bent toward her, fingers coiling in her hair, his breath coating her face. "Don't cheapen it. It's never like that between us."

"You're the one cheapening it."

"Ali…" He sounded distressed, at the end of his rope. "Please leave. I… I'm not in a place where I can handle this in the right way. I don't want to hurt you, *cara mia*."

"Then don't hurt me. Don't dismiss me as if I'm a nuisance. The whole reason I risked the rush-hour traffic is to see you. You're upset about something. I get it. But being nasty to me is unfair. Maybe you're not used to relationships with give-and-take. But you don't get to order me around like I'm some disposable member of staff.

"You don't get to make me do all the emotional work, always. And just because I love you doesn't mean I'll let you walk all over me."

The effect of her ultimatum was ruined when tears filled her eyes. Pushing away from him, she angrily swiped at her cheeks. God, did he have any idea that he could destroy her with one harsh word?

She had almost reached the door when she heard him say, "Don't leave, Ali. Don't let me chase you away."

Hand on the knob, Ali stilled. Loving him did make her vulnerable, but not weak. She felt him at her back and the entirety of her being wanted to lean into his waiting arms, to take the only comfort he offered in his touch, to lose herself in the fire between them. "Don't. Touch me."

The sharp inhale of his breath, the stillness, conveyed his shock.

"*Mia dispiace*, Ali. It seems I'm always saying sorry to you. Turn around and look at me. Please."

She turned but couldn't manage to look at him. Instead, she made her way to the sitting area, took a bottle of water from the small refrigerator and gulped the cold water down. She found him sitting at the two-seater and chose a sofa opposite him. His mouth narrowed but he didn't say anything.

"Do you accept my apology?"

"I don't know," she said with a shrug. "I came because she's leaving, Dante, your mother's leaving in a few hours."

Any tenderness that had returned to his expression faded. His face became that stony mask again. "I know."

"I feel sorry for her. She seems so desperate to make a connection with you. I'd give anything to see Papa again, to tell him how sorry I am, to tell him that all I ever wanted was to love him, and to have his love in return. Can't you forgive her for whatever she's done? For yourself, at least? It's clear it hurts you to see her."

He didn't say anything for so long that Ali braced herself for another cutting remark. His gaze grew distant, tight lines fanning out from his face. *"Nessuno."* The refusal rang around the silence like a pistol shot. "I don't think it's even a matter of forgiving her because I don't feel anything for her. Even before my father was incarcerated for his crime, she cut all ties with him.

Took her maiden name again. Within months, she had married her second husband. She urged me to change my last name too."

The utter lack of emotion in his eyes terrified Ali. It seemed that he really wasn't acting from a place of anger but nothingness.

Forgetting all her vows to herself, she went on her knees in front of him and took his hands in hers. He was cold, as if the past hadn't quite left him. "It makes her weak, yes, but not a monster, Dante."

"But he did it all for her. He was so in love with her, he so desperately wanted to please her that he cooked the books, embezzled from hundreds of innocents."

Ali fell back onto her haunches. "What?"

"She's from a wealthy Sicilian family with old ties to Mafia. He was a humble accountant. My mother… on the outside, she's a delicate flower but on the inside, she's spoiled, privileged. She is insidious with her demands, with what she thinks is her due. She was in a rebellious phase when she met him and he fell hard for her.

"Soon, I came and then reality descended on her. There were no cars, no villas, no jewelry, nothing exciting about being a mother at twenty-two. She grew up like royalty. Her discontent was like cancer and he…for her, he was determined to do anything. Which he did. Our wealth grew exponentially over a few years. Cars, mansions, a jet-setting lifestyle, he lay everything at her feet, her utter slave.

"I'm not justifying the number of innocent lives he ruined but *dios mio*, even at the end, he didn't regret it."

"You can't blame her for what he did. They were both weak." Fury filled her for between them they had distorted his view of love. And for that, she didn't want to forgive either of them.

He looked down at Ali, frowning. "You're right. It was his lack of a moral compass. But every time I see her, I can't forget that after everything, she didn't even have compassion for him, much less love. He rotted in that jail cell and when she refused to even visit him... When he heard that she'd married again, he hanged himself."

He rubbed his forehead with his fingers, and Ali's heart ached for him.

"When I see her, I remember his face. He was such a fool in love. To this day, I can't understand how a sensible man could lose himself like that. His love for her was his biggest weakness. It led to the destruction of countless others and himself. It's poison..." he said in a voice that was so full of bitterness that Ali thought she might choke on it.

Dante thought love was poison. A weakness. She felt as if someone had dropped a huge boulder on her chest, crushing the very breath out of her.

She had known he didn't believe in love. But to think of it as poison...

When he pulled her up, Ali went into his embrace and buried her face in his chest. "She doesn't deserve your tears, Ali. Or your sympathy." He seemed to hesitate, his mouth buried in her hair. "You were right. I don't do well with emotions. I will learn, *tesoro*, to be a good husband, to communicate with you. Never to hurt you like that again. We'll have a good marriage based on mutual respect and passion. When the time is right, we'll have a big family, if that's what you want. But you should know…" A tremor coated his words. "I will never allow myself to feel like that, never put my faith, my life in the hands of love. I can't change for you. I can't be anything other than what you see. Don't ask it of me."

Having dealt her that soft but final statement, he left her standing alone in what used to be her papa's office, her heart breaking softly.

For the young man who'd never had the chance to believe that love wasn't always a poison, or cancer. For a young man who didn't understand that even as he wreaked immense hurt on her, she still loved him with every molecule of her being.

That she could no more stop loving him, that she couldn't stop hurting for him any more than she could stop breathing.

Dante returned home that night, feeling like the lowest of the low.

His feet automatically took him to the guest room. His mother had left then. He stood in the center of it, the faint scent of gardenias filling his nostrils. For as long as he could remember she'd worn that scent. For as long as he could remember, she'd been a fragile beauty with no spine, letting the world sway her back and forth.

And to think he'd once assumed Ali was a spoiled princess like her and Francesca. He'd called her a pampered princess, once he'd even called her a waste of space.

No, his wife was a lioness with a heart of gold. And he'd hurt her tonight.

Unable and unwilling to face her reaction to his blunt words, he had left her alone in his office.

Dios mio, he couldn't bear to hurt her any more than he could love her. And the warring instincts constantly ate away at him.

She had come to offer comfort and he'd crushed her heart. But seeing his mother these past few weeks, dealing with the guilt in her eyes, reliving the worst years of his life all over again…he felt as powerless as that sixteen-year-old.

Left with the legacy of his father's crime and his death.

Left with discovering how, through the weakness they called love, they had fractured their family, his faith in them, his faith in everyone and everything.

For all the billions he'd amassed, for all the stains he'd removed from his reputation, Dante felt like a jerk, a weak man unable to stop wreaking hurt on the one woman who thought him worthy of her adoration, who refused to stop looking at him as if he were a hero.

He'd had Izzy schedule the meeting on a different floor, hiding away like a coward. Not that he'd been able to focus on a single word.

Maledizione! Enough was enough. He didn't intend to let the past rot his future with its poisonous fingers. He and Ali, against all odds, had made a fresh start and he intended to have a full life with her.

He would spend his life earning that adoration in her eyes. He meant for them to be consumed by the fire between them, again and again. For it was the one place where he could give of himself completely.

A sudden desperation gripping him, he checked the room she'd occupied when she'd moved in. There was no way he was going to let her spend the night in a different bed. She belonged with him. He switched on the lights in that room and found the bed neatly made, bare of any of her things.

Panic like he'd never known unfurled in his belly. Had she left him? Had he broken her heart? By the time he walked to his bedroom, his heart was thudding against his rib cage.

The bedroom door swung open wide and there she was in the middle of his bed, illuminated by a pool of light. Tenderness and relief and desire, a knot of emotions crowded in his throat. There was a rational voice crowing too but he couldn't even hear it.

She lay on her tummy, her leg splayed, her round buttocks thrust up, her face to the side, taking up most of the bed, as she always did. Moving to her side, he pushed the silky strands from her back and placed his palm on there. Just touching her calmed the wild need inside him. Just breathing in the scent of her, of seeing her in his bed night after night…desire crawled through him, sinuous and hard, as it always did.

He stripped and crawled into bed. Fear beat a tattoo in his head that he was far too deep already. But it didn't stop him from kissing the smooth skin of her back.

From shifting the thick curtain of her hair to the side

until he could kiss the shadows under her eyes. Shadows he knew he had put there.

From inhaling the scent of her deep into his lungs until she was a part of him.

From drawing a wet trail of kisses down to the round globes of her buttocks.

From turning her lithe body to the side until her back was resting against his chest.

From slipping one arm under her heated flesh until he reached the round fullness of her breast.

From rubbing his cheek against hers, against her shoulder, every inch of her he could reach like a starving man.

From whispering a torrent of mindless Italian at her ear, from threats to promises to pleading.

From smiling when she woke up with a soft mewl and when her sleep-mussed eyes alighted on his.

From saying "I'm sorry" a hundred times.

From the hardness in his chest melting when her mouth curved into a soft, welcoming smile.

From rubbing her plump nipple back and forth between his fingers.

From growling when she pressed herself into his touch wantonly.

From kissing the graceful curve of her neck.

From digging his teeth into the soft muscle of her shoulder.

From growling like a Neanderthal when she pressed her bottom into his groin, rubbing against him, until he was rock hard again.

From peeling her panties away from her legs like a man possessed.

From the utterly masculine grunt that escaped his throat when her wetness coated his fingers.

From nudging her upper leg up and away, from opening her wide for him, from pushing into her wet heat and lazily thrusting up into her until the restless beast in him calmed again.

From trailing his other hand down her silky body until it reached her clit.

From whispering, "Yes, again, *cara mia*," like a man possessed when she pleaded with him that her sensitive flesh couldn't clench and fracture again after her first release.

From the desperate need that crawled through his legs toward his spine when she turned and looked into his eyes, and said against his plundering mouth, "You can be selfish, Dante. You can take me once without thinking of my release. I'm more than happy for you to use me for your pleasure. As you want it, whenever, wherever."

From his chest cracking wide open.

From the cold sweat that claimed his skin as he worked his fingers and himself in tandem, determined that she would fly with him again.

And when she came with his name on her lips, and her muscles clenching and releasing around him like a silken glove, he couldn't stop himself from pushing her facedown onto the bed, from pulling her up onto all fours and thrusting into her from behind.

He couldn't stop his heart from aching, his body from shuddering again and again when she turned toward him, an impish smile around her mouth and said,

"Harder, Dante. Deeper, please. I want to come again. With you."

He had no idea how he managed to bring her to climax again. All he knew was that she fell apart and he lost even the semblance of control. For the first time in his life, nothing mattered but his own release. Nothing mattered but the burn riding up his thighs and pooling in his balls.

Nothing mattered except losing himself inside her. Hands fisted in her hair, teeth sinking into her shoulder, he drove in and out of her, working himself to the edge.

His climax when it came was the most powerful thing he'd ever experienced. The most raw, honest, revelatory moment in all his life. The most he had ever shared of himself, the most he had ever taken of someone.

He flopped onto her body, resting his weight on his elbows, his harsh breaths making her hair fly under him, their sweat-slicked bodies gliding and sliding against each other. Still, he wasn't satisfied. She was so fragile, so delicate beneath him. "Ali, look at me."

Hoarse. Raw. Uncivilized. Each word of his felt different. Felt new. He felt different. Somehow less, not enough for her.

She turned, her chin resting against the white sheets. Her hair flew away from her face as she blew at it, and then, after the spine-tingling experience they had just had, after the rough way he had used her, somehow she managed to smile at him. A gloriously warm smile that made her eyes shine and her mouth wide. "Hi."

A single, weightless word that lit up an incandescent joy in his chest.

When he finally noticed the uneven rhythm of her breath, he tried to move off her.

She shook her head.

"I'll crush you," he whispered, undone by the smile, by the warmth. By her.

"Not just yet."

"I'm sorry for earlier. For…leaving you like that."

"As long as you find your way back to me, we're okay, *si*?"

"*Si.*"

And then she tugged his head down to her and took his mouth in a wet, open, raw kiss that made him semi-hard between their bodies again. Her smile was pure wickedness. "That was fantastic, mind-blowing. You give good sex, babe. You're always worth the wait."

Like a teenage boy, he could feel himself blushing. He rubbed his thumb over her lip. "I didn't hurt you?"

"No, but it's your turn to compliment me. I know how fabulous I am but a girl needs compliments now and then."

He knew she was teasing but he couldn't laugh. He couldn't imagine life without her now. He rubbed his fingers over her shoulder and placed a reverent kiss to her damp skin. Emotion was hard for him, and words to express what he felt, even harder. "I'm glad I black-mailed you."

She flipped herself onto her back under him, and the rasp of her breasts against his chest made them both groan. And then her hands clasped his cheeks, her eyes shining. "I'm glad I caved."

With that simple statement, she rolled over to her

side, pulled his arm over to kiss his palm and nestled into him as if she belonged there.

His wife was the bravest woman he'd ever met. And he, a powerful, arrogant thirty-six-year-old who ruled his life with precise ruthlessness, was terrified of what else she would unleash on him.

Of what else she would ask of him that he couldn't, wouldn't be able to give. Of what he'd do the day she realized that finding his way back to her simply wasn't enough.

CHAPTER ELEVEN

ALISHA STARED AT her reflection in the mirror, her eyes wide at the outrageously sexy outfit she'd chosen for the party tonight.

And this dress she'd had specially commissioned from an up-and-coming British-Indian designer was it. It was an extravaganza for a woman who'd lived in jeans and T-shirts for a decade but Ali wanted to make her parents proud tonight.

She wanted the world to know of her happiness.

She wanted to share it with these people who'd been part of Matta Steel for generations.

She wanted to embrace her part in her papa's legacy.

She wanted Dante to be proud to call her his wife.

The wide, ruffled skirt of her mauve *lehenga* had layers upon layers of ruffles, giving her the fairy-tale princess look that was all the vogue on the runway this year. But the true genius of the outfit was in the *choli* and the *dupatta*.

When the designer, Maya, had showed the sketch to Ali, her first impulse had been a resounding no. It bared too much, it was too risqué. As far as she knew, a traditional *choli lehenga* was a wide, full skirt with a blouse that bared her midriff, yes, but covered everything up front with a silky *dupatta* to trail from her shoulder.

But since Ali had asked for a modern take on it, for something that was traditional and yet looked sensual, Maya insisted she give it a chance. And when Ali had tried it on, it had looked simply stunning.

The blouse was strapless with gossamer mauve sleeves hanging low on her arms leaving her entire neck and shoulders bare. But the silky blouse cupped her breasts from beneath, like a lover's hands, leaving the upper curves bare. Since she didn't have big boobs, it wasn't so much the cleavage that was outrageous but the way it covered only the lower half.

The *dupatta*, which was a silky shawl in the same mauve, shimmered with intricate silver thread work, hung from one shoulder.

At Ali's insistence, Maya had hitched it across her chest and pinned it to the skirt. So the effect was the mirage of the *dupatta* covering her torso on one side while her breasts played peekaboo on the other.

Big chandelier earrings hung from her ears while she left her hair down to show off the new haircut. She had made her eyes up into a subtly smoky kohl look and had dusted dark blush onto her cheeks. A light pink shimmering gloss on her lips and she was done.

She was ready to meet the world.

And she was ready to meet her husband whom she hadn't seen in three weeks.

She had so much news to share with him, so many

plans to make, so many things to look forward to that she felt as if she was bubbling over with happiness.

Ali had wanted to shock and surprise Dante but she was the one who got the surprise of the century as she stepped out of the chauffeured Mercedes that evening.

Matta Mansion glittered like a new bride on the night of the Diwali party, decorated with hanging lights everywhere. Focus lights from the grounds made the white marble facade glitter like an Indian palace of old. The gardens beyond had been decorated with fairy lights, every brass and copper artwork that had been the highlight of her mom's art collection polished to a sheen.

Ali walked into the ballroom and gasped. Thousands of red, earthenware *diyas* with cotton wicks had already been lit and cast shadows on walls. She had no idea how Dante's staff had managed to lay their hands on so many of them. No idea how he'd found out all the lovely Hindu traditions that surrounded the festival of Diwali and had them implemented. Especially when he'd been in Tokyo for three weeks.

A small trio of players were seated on a divan behind the main dais, decorated with flowing silks, playing *shehnai* and *tabla*. The scent of fresh flowers filled every nook and cranny. Just the delicious aroma of all the sweets the chefs had laid out on the massive buffet table had her mouth watering.

Ali stood on the second-floor balcony and looked out over the gardens. In another hour, every inch of space would be crammed with guests Dante had insisted they invite. Dusk was just an hour away. Once everyone was here, Dante would welcome them all.

They would light some sparklers and then there would be a feast.

Tears filled her eyes as unbidden, a memory came to her, drowning her.

Of her mama decorating the house just like this when Ali had been maybe four. Of throwing open the doors to every member of staff and employee of Matta Mansion. Of dressing Ali and Vikram in traditional clothes while she herself had worn a bright red sari and the diamond necklace that Alisha now owned. Of her papa picking her up and then kissing her mama on the forehead.

"Ali?"

Ali turned so fast that she almost tripped on the hem of her *lehenga*.

Dressed in a conservative black suit with a white shirt underneath, Dante looked suave and powerful and utterly masculine. Air left her lungs in a hurried rush. The platinum cuff links she had left for him on his study table glimmered at his cuffs. That unruly hair was combed back, highlighting the harsh features, rendering him absolutely magnificent.

"You look…incredible."

The husky, rough tone of his words made butterflies flutter in her belly. Suddenly, she was glad she'd gone with Maya's outrageous creation.

His hands landed on her shoulders, the rough pads of them slithering against her bare skin. Dark eyes studied her with lingering intensity. His gaze moved from her hair to her shoulders, lingering for just a few seconds on the way the *choli* cupped her breasts. Her nipples tightened, her blood thick as honey in her veins.

"I should have believed you when you said I'd be floored, Alisha." The way he said her full name made her smile. Exasperation coated his words. "Asking me to foot the bill for that dress is tricking me. It bares too much, Ali."

"It's called a *lehenga*," she said swishing the wide skirt in her hands with a brazen smile. "I told the designer to make it the most spectacularly sexy outfit London has seen in a while. I told her it should befit the wife of a gorgeous, arrogant, wonderful husband. I told her the world should remember the night when Alisha Matta—"

"Vittori."

She blinked. "What?"

"Alisha Vittori. You're Alisha Vittori. Not Matta anymore."

Alisha Vittori.

It was just a name, and yet her heart thudded against her rib cage.

She scrunched her nose and his jaw tightened. "Nobody really changes their name these days."

"Mrs. Puri, in all her omniscience, it seems, was right. I find I'm a traditionalist at heart. I want my wife to take my name. I want the entire world to know that, while you have me wrapped around your finger, I have a claim on you too. I never want there to be a doubt about why I want you as my wife."

The voices downstairs floated away leaving Dante

and her alone in their own world. His finger rubbed her collarbone, relentless heat spewing from the small touch.

With a groan, he covered her mouth with his. Completely. Utterly. The kiss was tenderness itself. Soft. Inviting. Opening up the whole world and putting it at her feet.

It seemed as if it was the very essence of the man he was—full of depth beneath the isolation he set upon himself, full of emotion and passion that he was determined to deny. A heart so big and that gave generously while remaining closed off to receiving anything in return.

He venerated her with those soft lips, his eyes shining because she'd given him everything. He knew it, she knew it. The words didn't need to be said. It was as she'd guessed—the only way into Dante's heart, the only way to carve a small place for herself in there, was to surrender everything. To lay everything open at his feet.

She felt as if she was stripped to flesh and bone, all her armor falling away. As if his kiss was what she was made for.

He deepened the kiss, his fingers in her hair, his hold on her heart tightening.

It spoke of things he would never say. It showed her that she had a place in his heart too, however small. It told her that this arrogant, powerful man was no more in control of the bond between them than she was.

He kissed her as if she were the most precious thing he had ever held. He extracted a tiny velvet box from his jacket and her heart raced.

TARA PAMMI   185

Every inch of her trembled as he pulled out a delicate-looking necklace. Three diamonds glittered in the middle of the thin chain, while tiny black beads lined up on either side. Ali stood, stunned, as he pushed her hair back and hooked the delicate chain behind her neck. It was a *mangalsutra*, the chain a husband put on his wife in the Hindu tradition.

His fingers lingered at her nape, his chin resting on her head.

She kept her head bowed, fighting the tears prickling behind her eyes. Fighting for breath. Struggling to stay still while the ground rocked from under her.

As if he understood, he wrapped his arms around her and held her tight. Her breasts pressed against his chest, her trembling legs held by the cradle of his powerful thighs.

"Mrs. Puri told me that I wasn't being fair. That your father would have demanded that I do right by you. That I was doing everything by my family's traditions, leaving yours out."

"She called you and took you to task?" Ali demanded. "She worships the ground you walk on."

The few seconds he waited resonated with his reluctance. "I called her and asked her to explain how things had been done with your parents. And she walked me through them. Ali, if you want a Hindu wedding or a reception, or a *mehendi* night or a bachelorette party, whatever you want, I want you to have it. I don't want you to resent me ten years down the line because I cheated you out of some tradition or custom. I don't want you to tell me in thirty years that I didn't give you a bride's trousseau as custom demands. I want you to have everything you desire, *cara mia*."

He had the whole mansion looking like it had during her childhood. Like a beautiful bride waiting for her groom.

He had decided that they would resurrect the tradition of the Diwali party, which had been her mother's yearly extravaganza. He'd invited so many of the old staff, Matta employees, charity workers, even Jai.

He had asked Mrs. Puri so that he could do right by her family's traditions.

And he claimed, again and again, that he had no heart to give. That he wasn't a romantic. That he didn't do relationships. That he didn't do love. Her heart seemed to have crawled into her throat and lodged there. Making even breathing difficult.

"Look at me, Alisha," he said in that commanding tone of his.

Chin quivering, Ali did. If he kissed her, she would melt into him. He was everything she had ever wanted and she felt as if she were in some fairyland where all her wishes were being granted. Terror filled her when she thought of that midnight stroke that would return everything back to reality, to a world without him.

"Will you be my wife, Ali?"

She took his hands in hers, tears running down her cheeks, and brought his hand to her cheek. "I don't need ceremonies to define this thing between us. The first time I walked into your bedroom, I became your wife, Dante. You're making me cry and I look like something the cat dragged in when I cry...and—oh, no, my makeup," she wailed.

Laughing, he produced a handkerchief and carefully blotted her cheeks. "You're always beautiful and it will drive me insane the whole evening that other men will see you in that outfit."

"Did Mrs. Puri tell you that according to Hindu traditions, you're stuck with me for seven lifetimes?"

He nodded and there was such tenderness in his eyes that it stole her breath. "I'm hoping that this is the first one. Shall we go down?"

"It's not fair," she whined.

He frowned. "What's not fair?"

"It's been three weeks and I'm dying to get you into bed, or against the wall, and there are all these people waiting for us..."

He pressed a chaste kiss to her temple as if to tease her even more. "Patience, *tesoro*. Remember, good things come to those who wait."

And he was worth the wait.

By the time they had seen the last guest off and were riding the elevator toward Dante's penthouse, it was past one in the morning.

Ali was so tired she felt like she could fall asleep standing up.

His arm around her shoulders, Dante pulled her to his side until all her weight was against him. His mouth was soft at her temple. And then he nuzzled her throat, the gesture less sexual and more tender. "Bed for you, I think. I've been waiting all evening to get you out of your...*lehenga*," he said gingerly, trying out the word, "but I'll do it to put you to bed."

Ali smiled so widely that she thought her mouth would crack. "No, no, no. I have a million things to tell you, plans to make for us and it's been killing me to wait."

His gaze lingered on the shadows under her eyes. "Ali, we can do it tomorrow morning. I'm not going anywhere."

"Please, Dante."

He laughed and pressed a swift kiss to her mouth. "Well, if you ask nicely like that, *si.*"

Excitement replacing the exhaustion, Ali hit the number for the floor to her studio. "First thing on the agenda for tonight—do you want to see my work?"

The anticipation and the pure joy that filled his eyes made him look breathtakingly beautiful. "*Si*, please."

She took his hand and dragged him with her. Just as they reached the door to the studio, she halted. "Actually, that's not the first item."

"Ali, I hate that I've made you so insecure with my cruel words, but please, *cara mia.*"

"No. It's not that. I...I just... I came up with this during the party."

His smile disappeared. "No, you can't be friends with Jai. I had Izzy invite him because you said he was looking for capital for his start-up and it would be good for him to network and meet some of the shareholders. It's not that I don't trust you, it's just that your ex in your life is not something I can tolerate. Please don't—"

She wanted to argue just for the heck of it. But Dante

was taking tentative steps toward communicating his feelings with her and really, she didn't even want Jai in her life. They had nothing in common anymore. Instead she said, "Okay. I won't."

He looked so shocked by her easy acceptance that she laughed out loud.

"Just like that?"

Going on her toes, she whispered, "Today's your lucky day, mister." She swiped her tongue over his lower lip until he opened for her. "I hope you take complete advantage of it. Of me." His answer was to kiss the hell out of her, until she forgot her own name.

He was panting when he pulled away, lust etched on every inch of his face. "If you want me to listen to all the items on your agenda, you had better keep your hands to yourself, *cara mia*."

Out of breath herself, Ali nodded.

It took her several minutes to retrace their conversation. "So, the first thing is that today, I... Having the party at the mansion, it made me realize...I want to live there. I mean, us, I want us to live there. To make our home there, make it a happy place again, fill it with good memories and laughter and..." She swallowed the word *love* at the last second.

"I think it would have made both Mama and Papa and even Vikram happy, don't you think? We can—" heat swarmed her cheeks at the intensity of his gaze "—like you said, when we're ready, we... I do want a big family and the grounds and the house would be perfect to raise an army of kids."

"An army?" he said in such a low voice that she laughed again.

"*Si.*"

"Okay. We'll live at Matta Mansion."

She took his hand and rubbed the palm against her cheek. Her heart was in danger of exploding out of her chest. "Just like that?" she said, trying to breathe over the lump in her throat.

"Today's your lucky day. I hope you take advantage of that, *bella mia.*"

I love you so much. The words flitted to her lips but Ali swallowed them away. She didn't want to bring awkwardness to such a beautiful day and she didn't want to make him uncomfortable.

Instead, she just nodded, took his hand and pulled him into her studio.

Dante had no idea what to expect. His disparaging comments before still shamed him. So he had forced himself to keep an open mind, to support and encourage her when she needed it, to catch her if she faced disappointment. Not because he thought she would fail but because art was such a subjective world and he just... he wanted to be there for her.

As Ali turned on the huge industrial-strength lights he'd had the workmen install when he had purchased two flats and had them converted into a large open studio for her, he told himself that whatever she showed him, he would praise her, he would encourage her effort. He would—

A number of blown-up framed photographs stood leaning against the walls all around him.

He found himself at an utter loss for words.

Each print was a candid shot—a starkly beautiful life moment captured in time. One was a naked woman in the kitchen of that restaurant in Bangkok—no hint of vulnerability in her face as she met the camera head-on. One was a woman feeding her child—utter bliss on her face. One was a man on his knees in front of a woman with his mouth on her sex, one of a woman covered in bruises from fingerprints on her neck to the impression of shoes on her belly and it went on and on and on.

Every single one of them was hauntingly beautiful, tender and yet real at the same time—life in all its glory and indignity—and each one spoke volumes of the extraordinary talent and perspective of the woman who had captured them.

Shame and pride warred within him, and still he had no words to say.

"Dante?" she whispered, no tentativeness or need for validation in her words.

Standing amid her black-and-white and color prints, she was a goddess.

He went to her, took her hands, kissed her knuckles. Searched his mind for the right words. *Cristo*, what could he say that would tell her how humbled he felt that she had shared them with him.

"I don't know why you did it, but thank you for buying me that camera all those years ago."

He shook his head, emotion clogging his throat.

"Don't…lay this at my feet, *bella*. If I hadn't, you'd have found another way to make it happen. You're… your work is…" he laughed. "Your papa…he would have been so proud, Ali. He would have been elated to see how extraordinary you are."

Tears overflowed in her eyes and fell down onto her cheeks. She came to him like lightning and fire and he caught her in his embrace. Held her while she cried. Glad that for once in his life, he'd found the right words to say to her.

Hoping that every time she came to him for something like this, he had enough to give her what she needed.

Hoping that, for the first time in his life, his past hadn't robbed him completely of his ability to give affection, to receive the love she gave him.

Ali had no idea how long she stayed in Dante's arms like that. All she knew was that life couldn't get more beautiful. Or more giving. He was so solid and real and wonderful in her arms that she never wanted to let go. The moment was so tender and loving and complete she almost changed her mind. Almost.

But she didn't want to start their new life hiding something so important from him. She didn't want to make this decision on her own. She shouldn't have to. Especially since it affected them both. And she was sure, whether he agreed with her or not, he would want to know.

So, as much as she wanted to stay in his arms and beg him to take her to bed, she took a long breath, filled her lungs with the essence of him and pulled back slightly. "Do I look all grungy then?" she said, still trying to find the right words. "I have too much makeup on to be crying every other second."

He didn't smile. A little line appeared between his brows, as if he knew she was delaying. But then, he did know her very well.

"What is the third thing on your agenda?"

She stepped out of his embrace completely and faced him. "My agent wants me to do an exhibit, as soon as possible, actually. Her team is trying to decide which gallery will display it best. And she told me that they're all trying to get it to theirs. It will start in London, and based on the reception, it might…go to other cities, like New York, Beijing. We're still talking about the details.

"It's all happening so fast. I've hired an employment agency and put out ads for employees for the charity too."

"That's fantastic news. The world should see your talent. And it looks like you're doing the best thing for the charity. You can still be involved at a higher level. Are you worried about the travel?"

Ali shook her head and swallowed the misgivings in her throat. "No, no… That's not it. It's just that something else has come up too. Do you remember that photography apprenticeship I had wanted to go on but that never happened?"

He didn't completely withdraw, but his mouth tightened. *"Si."*

Ali looked down at her laced fingers. Christ, why was this so hard? Why did it suddenly feel like there was an ocean between them already? "My agent showed some of my work to this American entrepreneur/philanthropist who puts together teams to work in some of the remotest areas of the world, like Tibet, Bosnia, Haiti. You know, sometimes they're war zones, sometimes it's just a re-building effort to clean up after natural disasters.

"Anyway, he got in touch with me a week ago, out of the blue. No introductions. Not his agent reaching out to mine. Just called me one afternoon when I was here and asked me if I could meet him in a couple of hours because he was leaving London that night.

"Two minutes into the meeting, he asked me to join his team on the next expedition. Apparently, he always hires a world-renowned photographer to capture the expedition, sort of to bring those things to the world's notice. My agent told me he's never asked anyone as young as me before, but apparently, when she forwarded some of my work to him, he instantly decided that he wanted me. I've been reading up all about his teams and the trips they take, and I realized what an honor it is to be chosen."

Dante covered the distance between them and hugged her tightly. "I'm not surprised."

Some of her tension dissolved. When he held her like that, it felt as if there wasn't anything she couldn't conquer. "Yeah?"

He tipped her chin up. "You didn't say yes?"

"No. I… First, I was just so stunned. It took me a while to realize what a big compliment it was to my work. Not until I Googled the hell out of him. And then that night, my agent asked me what I was waiting for.

I told her I'd have to talk to you. I mean, it's a decision that affects both of us, our life together and I… It didn't feel right to just say yes and then tell you about it afterward. I wanted to talk to you about it. It's been so hard to just sit on it while you were in Tokyo."

Once again, Dante had no words. He kept thinking he had the measure of her and she kept surprising him. His chest felt tight, as if his heart was too big for it. "Ali…" His hands shook as he gathered her to him. "I'm glad you waited to discuss it with me although it's not necessary. This is your career and I want it to go from height to height until the whole world takes pleasure in your work."

She nodded but her anxiety was like a cloak around her. He hated to see her smile dim. He pushed the hair back from her shoulder and covered the silky bare skin. "What is worrying you? Is there a fee you have to pay? Don't worry about finances or the charity."

"No, there isn't. Of course, I don't get paid either because it's a privilege to join his team."

"So what's the problem?"

"The next trip that he wants me to go on…will leave in a month."

"And?"

"I'll be gone for at least eighteen months. Might be more. If I agree and sign the contract, I'm bound by it. I can't just up and leave if I don't like it. Of course, there will be scheduled breaks but I'm told they won't be long."

It was like a punch to his stomach. He couldn't imagine not seeing her for eighteen months. *Cristo*, he felt like a teenager saying goodbye to his first crush. It felt like a lifetime. "I see," he said, just to give himself time to gather his fragmented thoughts.

Ali hid her face in his chest, as if afraid of his reaction. The graceful line of her profile, the small tremors he could feel in her shoulders… This was the opportunity of a lifetime.

He couldn't be selfish. Her commitment to their marriage, to him, it was more than he'd ever expected to have in life. She was more than he'd ever expected to have. "There's nothing to it but that you go. *Si*, it will be hard not to see each other for that long but I… I'm going nowhere. Our life together is going nowhere.

"Just don't…fall in love with some guy on this expedition." The words fell away before he could prevent them. He cringed at how pathetic and insecure he sounded. But there was no arresting that chain of thought. He pulled her left hand up, the diamond winking at him. "Remember that you belong to me, *cara mia*."

Brown eyes glared at him through thick lashes. "It's not funny, Dante. Do you really not trust me?"

He rubbed his thumb over her cheek, compulsively. "Of course I trust you. You're just…" He blew out a big breath. Damn it, he'd always been strong and he needed to be strong for her in this. He couldn't use her affection for him to sway her. She would come to hate him for it and he couldn't bear that.

"Eighteen months is a long time!" He slammed his head back. That was the exact opposite of what he meant to say.

"Exactemente!" Instead of looking upset, she nodded her head fiercely. "I was hoping you'd say that. I don't think I can go that long without seeing you. No, I know I can't. These two- and three-week trips to Tokyo have been bad enough." She nuzzled into his neck, and he felt the flick of her tongue at his throat. The bite of her teeth at his pulse. He hardened instantly against the soft curve of her bottom and she groaned. "I...was hoping you'd come with me."

Dios mio, when she moved like that, all he could think of was to be inside her. Eighteen months was a long time, his brain repeated the thing on a loop. It took him a couple of minutes to process her last sentence. "What?"

She pulled back so that she could look into his eyes. "You know, like a long honeymoon. Except instead of luxury hotels as you're used to, it will be tents or huts or whatever accommodation they give us. We wouldn't have to be apart at all. I checked with my agent and his team and they said spouses are welcome. Of course they'll expect you to pitch in, but I don't see that as a problem. That way eighteen months will just be a breeze and then we can return—"

"Stop, Alisha! Just...stop talking." He felt as if she'd knocked him down.

She turned those big eyes on him. Expectant. Wide. Full of hope and happiness.

But nothing could stop his answer. "I can't just take eighteen months off. I run a billion-dollar company."

"I know. I mean I'm sure you can stay in contact with your teams even in the remotest areas. The voting shares have been officially transferred so you don't have to worry about a coup or any such thing. Izzy told me how Uncle Nitin tried to sabotage the Japanese deal and how that forced you to finally put him on a leash. So he's not a worry anymore either."

Dante stiffened. "What Nitin almost got away with proves that I need to be at the helm. I can't just walk away."

She leaped out of his arms, as if being near him was unbearable. Shaking her head, clutching her midriff. As if he was supposed to agree instantly to her madcap idea. "No one's asking you to quit Matta Steel. I don't think what you do is easy or small. I know that thousands of livelihoods depend on the company. If you're willing to at least give this thought, I'm sure it'll be a matter of snapping your fingers to have the technology to support it ready."

Dante paced the floor, feeling as if there was some dark force coming at him but he couldn't do anything to avoid it. As if he was losing her, but there was nothing he could do to hold on to her.

What she was suggesting was…unthinkable. The company was everything to him. "I can't go away for eighteen months, Ali. I just can't. What you're suggesting is childish and… I understand you're excited and got carried away but it's not that simple."

"Ask me not to go then. This is a great opportunity to build my career, to bring exposure to my work, yes. But at the end of the day, it is only one way. Ask me to give it up for you, for us, for our marriage and I'll do it. I'll happily stay, Dante. Please, just ask me. Demand it of me."

"*No!* Don't do that, not for me. I don't deserve it. Damn it, Ali... I can't give you anything in return for such a sacrifice." The words piled out of his mouth, a strange tightening in his throat. It felt as if she was cutting his very breath off. Felling him at every turn. Like his heart was in her hand and she was fisting it tight.

"It's not a sacrifice, Dante. That's what you don't seem to understand. I love you. I want to spend my life with you. I want to make our marriage a priority. I just... Don't cut me down at every turn. Please, Dante."

He didn't want her sacrifice. It would choke him for the rest of their lives. "I can't ask you to set your career aside for me. For us."

Hurt made her stomach so tight that Ali felt as if she couldn't breathe. He wasn't even going to consider any option she presented. He refused to take a step toward her, and he forbade her from taking one toward him. She pulled at her hair, fear beating a tattoo in her veins. "So how does this work then? What if, after this trip, I go on another one? How will this marriage work then?"

"You're asking me hypothetical questions to which I have no answers. Matta Steel is my lifeblood. I can't shirk my responsibilities. I can't risk something I have given decades to."

"Won't or can't, Dante?" she said, anger coming to her rescue. "What's the point of being a bloody billionaire if you can't even be your own boss? What's the point of this marriage if we are together when it's convenient for your career and mine? When you won't let me give myself to it completely and neither will you? You would have us live in this strange…limbo just because you fear love?"

A cold frost filled his eyes, turning his gray eyes unbearably distant. Even cruel. He was a stranger again. A man she hated. A man who had not an ounce of tenderness in him. A man who cared about nothing but the company. "Don't make this small thing between us into a transaction, Alisha. Don't twist this into some sort of big, romantic gesture that I'm supposed to do for you to prove what you mean to me.

"You don't get to dictate how this marriage works. Now or in the future. I can't just step away from the company I've given everything to, from the role for which I married you in the first place. I'm not my father. I never will be."

She nodded, suddenly everything so clear to her naively wishful heart. "But I'm not asking you to make a big, romantic gesture. I'm not asking you to give up Matta Steel. I'm just…"

It wasn't that he wasn't even giving her idea a chance. It was the rigidity with which he did it. He'd always draw careful, clear lines between them. Always be a little out of her reach. Always decide what their relationship would be and would not be. Push him a little and he trampled her. Demand a little more than he wanted to give and he would crush her heart.

God, she'd been so stupid. She'd imagined them in some tent under the stars in some remote location, weaving an even stronger bond for life. She'd imagined having him all to herself. She'd built so many castles in the air.

The idea of walking away from their life together before it had even begun made her chest ache. "No. You won't even give this thing between us a chance. God, Dante, you don't even know how to take that I'm happy and what I'm willing to give. You're so terrified that I'll demand some price for not going. For simply loving you. What do I have to do to prove that I won't? How long will I have to worry what I say or do will make you think I'm asking something you can't give. That I'm asking too much of you. It will always be me reaching out. Always be me waiting for you to love me, maybe just a little."

"I can't... I won't be manipulated in this relationship, Alisha."

"Then there's nothing more to be said except goodbye."

"Ali—"

"I'm going back to the mansion. Don't come after me, please. Not tonight. I... I'll leave soon and it will provide you with the perfect excuse to tell your precious media. And don't worry, your reputation will be pristine, just like always. I won't tell the world I fell in love with a man who truly doesn't know the meaning of the word."

Every instinct in her clamored to wait for him. To let him catch her, to let him hold her, to let him chase away the pain in her heart. But he was the one breaking it. He was the one throwing it away, the one who didn't realize what her love truly meant. He would always measure it like a transaction, always think of it as a weakness.

She had put her world, her heart, at his feet. And he had simply kicked it away.

So she held her head high and went back to the elevator.

She'd lived alone before, she'd somehow made it through, and she would do it this time too. Even if it felt like the pieces of her were too many ever to mend again.

CHAPTER TWELVE

SHE WAS GONE.

She'd been gone for over a month.

First, she left the flat, bunking down one floor below him, in the studio he had had built for her. Because he'd been worried about what trouble she would get herself into, and he wanted to keep an eye on her. Because he'd thought Alisha was a liability he was taking on. And he would need to do damage control.

The first couple of days in the flat without her had been his first glimpse of hell. Memories of her seemed to have been absorbed into the very walls, the very fabric of his home.

He'd lived alone for countless years and yet the silence now had a different, haunting quality. So Dante had taken to sleeping at his suite at work.

Then she'd walked up to the flat one evening when he'd returned for a change of clothes.

Clad in that off-the-shoulder loose sweater and some kind of leggings, she'd looked so excruciatingly lovely that it had been a kick to his gut. "You cut your hair," he'd said, unable or unwilling to keep a possessive tone out of his voice.

She hadn't even called him on it. Fingering the wispy ends that framed her delicate face and highlighted those sharp cheekbones, she'd simply said, "It will be easier this way. I won't have time to wash and blow-dry."

And then she'd told him that she was packing up all her work, leaving it with her agent, and that she was leaving the studio too.

That all that open space he'd had custom-built for her, premium real estate in London, was free again, to do whatever he wanted with. He'd been so angry with her.

He had still not understood how she could make a mountain of a molehill, how she was using a small difference of opinion as an excuse to turn her back on her vows, to walk out of their life together.

It wasn't as if he had asked her to turn down that opportunity. It wasn't as if he had told her that he would not wait for her.

No, he hadn't begged, it wasn't in his makeup to do so. But, even in the fury that had gone through him, he'd said he was okay with the kind of life she had described for their future. That even if she chose to go on expedition after expedition, to build her career, to do what she loved, to follow her passion, that it was okay with him. That he would always be in London, that he would always have a place for her in his life.

She looked as if he had swung an arm at her. As if he was speaking in a different language. As if he was the one who didn't know the meaning of compromise.

It wasn't what he wanted out of their life together, it wasn't the picture he had of their marriage. He didn't want her to go off for long months at a time, leaving him behind. But, still, he had taken that step.

She'd looked like another word from him would blow her away, like a fluttering leaf, but she hadn't cried. Funnily enough, he would have felt better if she had cried. Instead, the emptiness in her eyes, the sheer absence of that light that was her spirit, had terrified him.

And then she moved into her papa's home. He knew she'd been there for three weeks before flying to New York to meet the philanthropist's team. He knew that in just a few days, she would leave for wherever it was that they were going.

Izzy had the information about their destination. He'd ordered her to get as much information as possible from Alisha, but had forbidden her to tell him where she was going. He didn't want to know. He didn't want to know in which part of the world his wife was.

But even after a month of her being gone, he was surprised at how empty everything felt each evening when he came home. He wasn't some romantic fool, some naive idiot in love to expect some kind of miracle to happen. He didn't expect her to be there waiting for him, in tank top and shorts, waiting to tease him, torment him, to love him.

Dios mio, how she had loved him. How she had touched him and kissed him and taken him inside her.

But every night he missed her. He missed her in his

bed. He missed her in the kitchen. He missed her in his heart.

So he'd done what he'd always done to protect himself when life dealt him a setback. He'd reminded himself he had what he had always wanted. He was the CEO of Matta Steel.

He had thrown himself into the Japanese merger, worked like a demon for eighteen, twenty hours a day, hitting the bed only when sheer exhaustion claimed his limbs. When he was so brain-dead that thoughts of Ali couldn't torment him. He'd waited to feel that knife edge of desire to wane. Waited for the day when he would wake up and not reach for her. Waited for him to stop expecting her to walk in. Waited to stop holding his breath for her to kiss him, claim him. Like only she did.

Today, this morning, was not that morning.

Tonight, it seemed, was not that night. Grabbing the keys to her studio, he took the elevator to the floor below. He had a feeling he had left sanity behind a few days ago. That he was on the very edge that he'd been determined all his life to avoid. That despite his every safeguard, despite him breaking her heart, Alisha had brought him to his knees.

He pushed open the door to the studio and turned on the industrial lights. Bare walls and empty floors greeted him.

There was no trace of her in the studio, just as she'd left no trace in the flat. A strange fever gripping him, he walked around until he felt as if the walls were closing in on him. And that was when he saw it, one lone print, framed, blown up, sitting against the far wall, covered by brown paper and tied together with string.

He was so desperate for a glimpse of her work, for a glimpse of her, that he realized he was tearing through the paper with no respect for her work. Breathing hard, he forced himself to slow down. Slowly, he removed the brown paper, picked up the frame and brought it to where he could see it properly.

What he uncovered stole the remaining breath from his lungs.

It was him.

His picture. The one she must have taken before he realized that she was taking pictures of him.

Before he'd been even completely awake. When he'd still been in that moment between sleep and wakefulness, when all his defenses were down, when his heart was as free and light as it had been when he'd been a small boy, loved by his parents.

It had been in that moment when he'd automatically reached out for her, searching for her. She'd zoomed in on his face at the second before he'd found that she wasn't there next to him. And somehow, she'd captured everything he felt for her but hadn't even known.

Such love, pure and complete, such anticipation, such expectation, such utter trust, that somehow when he reached for her, and when he found her, his life would be complete. That he would be complete.

What had she felt when she had developed the print? Why hadn't she come to him with it, why hadn't she shown him what he'd felt and demanded that he acknowledge it? Why hadn't she—?

It will always be me reaching out. Always be me waiting for you to love me, maybe just a little.

Dios mio, she had begged him to give them a chance. She'd asked him for one capsule of time in his entire life and she had promised to give him all of hers. All the moments, all of herself. And he had said no. He'd pushed her away. He'd called her childish, dramatic, he'd told her she was twisting things.

God, he didn't deserve her.

It wasn't his father's fault or his mother's fault, it was his own. He had had love like he had never known before and he had pushed her away. *Cristo*, he'd actually put the company before his wife.

She was right, he was a coward. He had known in his heart that she was everything to him. That if she persisted, she could demand his very soul and he would put it at her feet.

I will not be my father.

God, he'd even given voice to his biggest fear.

From the beginning, she had floored him with her generous heart. She'd captured him with her surrender and Dante found he had nowhere to go, no recourse but to tell the woman that stole his heart that he loved her.

That all the riches in the world didn't mean anything without her. That for her, he would give up a hundred companies, he would give up everything.

She was everything to him.

New York in December was like a page from a fairy tale.

White blankets of snow covered every building, every street, wherever Ali looked.

Christmas lights sparkled everywhere—on buildings, skyscrapers, trees, awnings of tall apartment buildings, reflected brightly on the white snow-covered ground.

But she'd never believed in fairy tales, not even as a child. Maybe that was what came of living with a single parent, of being the product of a failed marriage.

Even when the city was at its most beautiful, its most brilliant, Ali still saw the broken-down buildings, the cheap housing and poverty, a sharp contrast to the glittering beauty and opulence. She loved walking through the different boroughs, and she'd been going through the rolls on her camera like it was candy. It was such an interesting landscape. So much life to see. To capture.

But, every once in a while, especially when she was being jostled around by typical New Yorkers in Manhattan, suddenly she would spot a well-dressed man—usually in an expensive three-piece suit, his hair jet-black, his profile sharp—and just like that, her heart would crash to a complete stop.

The masses of people around her, the noise, the decadent scents of food and sometimes the nauseous scents of decay, the honk of horns, the chatter in different languages flying back and forth…everything would melt away. She'd still, even with the wind biting her cheeks, and crane her neck to locate that tall man. Every molecule in her body thrumming with hope that maybe, this time, it was not some stranger, not some executive, but Dante.

It happened a dozen times, a hundred times, and yet,

she fell for it every single time. Hope, excitement and then the crash of disappointment, followed by such a paralyzing ache in her chest.

She went through her day, meeting with John Carter's team, trying different restaurants in Manhattan and midtown, just living. Slowly, she would build herself back up and then she would spot someone again.

It was a vicious loop that she seemed to be stuck in.

She couldn't wait to leave New York. But Mr. Carter's assistant had only informed her this morning the trip had been indefinitely delayed.

No reason had been given and Ali, for once too distracted, hadn't even asked for it.

In the first week, she'd realized that the scale of these trips was beyond what she'd initially imagined. The logistics were mind-boggling. The question left to her was whether she should stay in New York or go back to London.

New York, her aching heart whispered immediately.

Because New York was an ocean away from him.

Because, as much as it pained her to keep looking for him in a crowd where he would never be, at the end of the day, she had lived through another day without breaking down. Without calling him just to hear his voice.

Without jumping onto a flight back to London to beg him to take her back. On whatever terms.

She couldn't do that. She couldn't always be the one reaching out. Couldn't live with the constant choke hold of worry about what would make him shut down.

Whereas London was full of memories. She wasn't

sure she even had the strength to walk away again. It had been hard enough to do it the first time. Pulling her coat together, Ali checked the street sign and sighed. Finally, she had made it to the Plaza.

She'd stay another week and then decide. Right now, it was time to join the living.

She forced herself to smile as she pulled the glass door open.

It wasn't Christmas yet but she knew Christmas parties abounded everywhere.

It would be nice to see the people she would be working with over the next eighteen months. It would be nice to forget the man she had left behind for at least a couple of hours.

She inquired at the reception desk and was directed to a suite on the twentieth floor.

Since the receptionist had immediately turned away to take a call, Ali swallowed her question and made her way to the bank of elevators. She checked her hair in the mirror and straightened the sweater dress she'd worn over black leggings.

In no time, she was knocking on the door. Something didn't feel right. She almost turned away just as the door opened and there was Dante.

A barrage of emotions came at Ali, knocking the very breath out of her. "What the hell are you doing here?"

But she didn't wait for his answer.

She turned away but didn't really make it far before he grabbed her arm and pulled her into the suite and closed the door behind her.

After two months, after searching for that beautiful face in every stranger, the sight of him rocked the ground from under her. Stole her breath. He was wearing a chunky sweater and dark jeans.

Two or three days' worth of beard covered his jaw, giving him a dangerous quality. Hiding that sensual mouth. His eyes glinted with some secret agenda, his shoulders stiff with tension.

In fact, he didn't look like the remote, coldhearted man she'd left behind at all. He looked distracted, rumpled, a little bit broken, as if he were human after all. As if despite his best efforts, she had left a little mark on him.

"*Buongiorno*, Alisha." His gaze swept over her sweater dress clinging to her breasts. A fire licked in his eyes. "You look good enough to eat, *cara mia*. I missed you. *Dios mio*, how I have missed you."

Even with the chill from outside still clinging to her skin, those husky words instantly warmed her up. The emotion ringing in them was a slap to her senses.

She wasn't going to engage with him. She wasn't going to get into a fight. She didn't want to spend a minute more than necessary with him, because at the rate her heart was beating, she was going to collapse on the bed and beg him to give her mouth-to-mouth. "I don't have anything to say to you. Nothing new to negotiate. In fact—" her throat filled with tears "—I take back what I offered. I won't give up this opportunity of a lifetime for you. You don't deserve it. You don't deserve me, Dante."

A bleakness entered his eyes. He ran a hand through

his hair, his only tell that he wasn't quite put together. "I deserved that."

"Stop agreeing with me. Stop telling me you missed me. Just…stop."

"Don't cry, *cara mia*. I promised I wouldn't hurt you. I just want a conversation with you. Just half an hour of your time, Ali. Then you can walk out of here. I won't stop you."

Slowly, the shock of seeing him faded, and reality sank in. "Wait, I don't understand. How are you here?"

"I took the jet this morning."

Why was he playing with her like this? Letting her tote fall down to the floor, she leaned against the bed. She rubbed a hand over her forehead. "Why are you here, at the Plaza? John's assistant told me the team was meeting for Christmas drinks."

"That was me. I had John postpone the trip too."

Shock pulsed through her. "What? Why?"

"I had a lot of things to see to. Paperwork…"

"Paperwork, of course. What is it this time, Dante? What else requires signing? What else do you want from me? Because I have nothing left to give you. Nothing."

"Ali, I know I've—"

"This is not fair. I…I can't do this again and again. I can't walk away from you over and over. Don't play games with me."

"I've never played games with you. Not once. Not even in my dreams."

His fingers clasped her chin in a firm hold, his eyes boring into her. He studied her as if she were dessert after a fast. As if he were parched for the taste of her. "I…told John that I want to join the team. But I need a month or two at least to get things in good shape at the company. I can't just… If I need to give this my all— and I desperately want to—I need to make sure there are contingencies in place, in case the teams can't get to me immediately.

"I made three trips to Tokyo to make sure there were no problems with the production line. He twisted my arm of course, until I made a huge donation. But like you said, what's the whole point of being a billionaire if you can't bribe your wife's boss to wait until you can beg her forgiveness? To wait so that I can join her before she disappears for eighteen months and leaves my heart broken? Because it has been, *cara mia*. Without you…"

Hands on her hips, he dragged her to him until she was pressed up against him from chest to thighs. Shaking and shuddering, he was a fortress of heat and desire around her. Relief, it was relief that gripped him, she realized. "I kept dreaming that you had left before I could get to you. I've never felt so powerless…not since the *polizia* came to take Papa away. You were right. What I suggested wasn't a compromise at all. *Dios mio*, one eighteen-month stint is bad enough. If you left me like that again… I'm sorry for not realizing the value of what you gave me. I'm sorry for hurting you so much. For being so…"

His mouth trailed soft kisses all over her face, down her jaw, onto her neck until her pulse was in his lips. Shock and pleasure and hope—all collided with each other in her chest, vying for the upper hand.

Pleasure won and she clung to him like a limp doll, willing him to take her mouth without having to beg for it. Rough hands snuck under her blouse, branding her bare skin.

Words came and fell away from her mouth and Ali stared, hope fluttering its wings in her chest.

She gasped when Dante sank to his knees and buried his face in her belly. Dark eyes, shimmering with wetness, looked up at her. "I'm going with you, just not immediately. Do this trip and return to London or not. Do a hundred trips for the rest of our lives and don't return to London. I don't care. As long as we're together."

"Are you sure? This is not a transaction." A sob racked through her. "It's not a condition to love you. To be with you. It's not... If you ask me to leave with you to return to London today, now, I will. I just... I need to love you in my own way, Dante. Even if you don't. Even if you—"

When she would have interrupted him, he nipped her, effectively silencing her. "I'm in love with you, *cara mia*. We will travel the world so that you can take more of those powerful photographs. We will live like nomads if that's what you want. Our kids will travel with us if that's what you want. We'll never return to London again. Never buy a home. We'll do it all your way."

Ali sank to her knees and burrowed into him. "No. All I wanted was for you to take a step toward me. To let me love you like I want to. To love me back just a little."

"I love you a lot," he said and utter joy spread through her.

"I will make my home with you, wherever you are, Dante. You're my home, don't you see? Always, you've been the place I can land, the person I can love. You're everything to me."

Dante picked his wife up in his arms, his heart bursting with love for his wife.

* * * * *

If you enjoyed
Sicilian's Bride for a Price
you're sure to enjoy these other
Conveniently Wed! *stories!*

Blackmailed by the Greek's Vows
by Tara Pammi
Bound to Her Desert Captor
by Michelle Conder
The Greek's Bought Bride
by Sharon Kendrick
Claiming His Wedding Night Consequence
by Abby Green
Bound by a One-Night Vow
by Melanie Milburne

Available now!

COMING NEXT MONTH FROM

HARLEQUIN
Presents®

Available November 20, 2018

#3673 THE ITALIAN'S INHERITED MISTRESS
by Lynne Graham
Isla has escaped to her recently inherited Sicilian villa, and the
last person she expects to see is the billionaire who changed
her life irrevocably. Alissandru wants what's rightfully his—Isla's
inheritance. But what he wants more is Isla...back in his bed!

#3674 MARRIED FOR HIS ONE-NIGHT HEIR
Secret Heirs of Billionaires
by Jennifer Hayward
Santo's stunned to see Giovanna again. Why, after that one
forbidden night, did she leave? But when Gia reveals their secret
consequence, the Italian will claim his son—and Gia as his wife!

#3675 CLAIMING HIS CHRISTMAS WIFE
Conveniently Wed!
by Dani Collins
After their marriage ended in heartbreak, Travis never wanted to
see Imogen again. But to avoid a scandal, they must agree to a
temporary reconciliation—leaving Travis tempted to reclaim his
wife...for good!

#3676 BOUND BY THEIR CHRISTMAS BABY
Christmas Seductions
by Clare Connelly
To legitimize his son, Gabe knows he must marry Abby—the
innocent beauty he shared a steamy festive night with! But can
their marriage be in name only, or will red-hot chemistry take over?

HPCNM1118RA

#3677 AN INNOCENT, A SEDUCTION, A SECRET

One Night With Consequences

by Abby Green

When Seb spies Edie's talent for lavish interior decoration, he makes an irresistible job offer—spend the festive season decorating his opulent home! But soon, Edie becomes the sensual gift Seb wishes to unwrap...

#3678 THE BILLIONAIRE'S CHRISTMAS CINDERELLA

by Carol Marinelli

Abe Devereux is famed for his cold heart. So meeting Naomi, who's determined to see the good in him, is a novelty. But will seducing her be his biggest risk, or his greatest chance of redemption?

#3679 PREGNANT BY THE DESERT KING

by Susan Stephens

Lucy is shocked by Tadj's royal revelation: Lucy is carrying the baby of a desert king! Tadj will secure his heir, but can Lucy accept his scandalous solution—that she share his royal bed?

#3680 THE VIRGIN'S SICILIAN PROTECTOR

by Chantelle Shaw

Hired to keep heiress Ariana safe, wealthy bodyguard Santino is intrigued by her hidden vulnerability. Their sexual tension is electric! And when Santino discovers just how innocent Ariana is, resisting her temptation becomes an impossible challenge...

Get 4 FREE REWARDS!

We'll send you 2 FREE Books plus 2 FREE Mystery Gifts.

Harlequin Presents® books feature a sensational and sophisticated world of international romance where sinfully tempting heroes ignite passion.

FREE
Value Over
$20

*Santo's stunned to see Giovanna again. Why, after
that one forbidden night, did she leave? But when Gia
reveals their secret consequence, the Italian will claim
his son—and Gia as his wife!*

*Read on for a sneak preview of
Jennifer Hayward's next story,*
Married for a One-Night Consequence.

He set his glass down with a clatter. "I am his *father*. I
have missed three years of his life. You think a *weekend
pass* is going to suffice? A few dips in the Caribbean as he
learns to swim?" He fixed his gaze on hers. "I want *every
day* with him. I want it *all*."

"What else can we do?" she queried helplessly. "You
live in New York and I live here. Leo is settled and
happy. A limited custody arrangement is the only realistic
proposition."

"It is *not* a viable proposition." His low growl made
her jump. "That's not going to work, Gia."

She eyed him warily. "Which part?"

"All of it." He waved a Rolex-clad wrist at her. "I
have a proposal for you. It's the only one on the table,
nonnegotiable on all points. Take it or leave it."

The wariness written across her face intensified. "Which is?"

"We do what's in the best interests of our child. You marry me, we create a life together in New York and give Leo the family he deserves."

Don't miss
Married for a One-Night Consequence,
available December 2018 wherever
Harlequin Presents® books and ebooks are sold.

www.Harlequin.com

HPEXP1118

HARLEQUIN

Presents®

Coming next month—a festive trio just in time for the holidays!

Claiming His Christmas Wife by Dani Collins

Part of the Conveniently Wed! miniseries

When Imogen faints in the cold New York snow, Travis is called to his ex-wife's very public rescue! But, with a deal *just* for Christmas, will he be able to let Imogen go a second time?

Bound by Their Christmas Baby by Clare Connelly

Part of the Christmas Seductions miniseries

When brooding bachelor Gabe learns Abby is his business rival's daughter, he's furious. So what will he do when she returns the following Christmas with their secret baby?

The Billionaire's Christmas Cinderella by Carol Marinelli

Tycoon Abe is overwhelmed by the potency of his undeniable connection with Naomi. Now he wants this shy Cinderella between his sheets by Christmas!

Available December 2018

Want to give in to temptation with
steamy tales of irresistible desire?

Check out **Harlequin® Presents®**,
Harlequin® Desire and
Harlequin® Kimani™ Romance books!

New books available every month!

CONNECT WITH US AT: